MAXIM: OBEY

A CLUB XXX NOVEL: BOOK TWO

LANA SKY

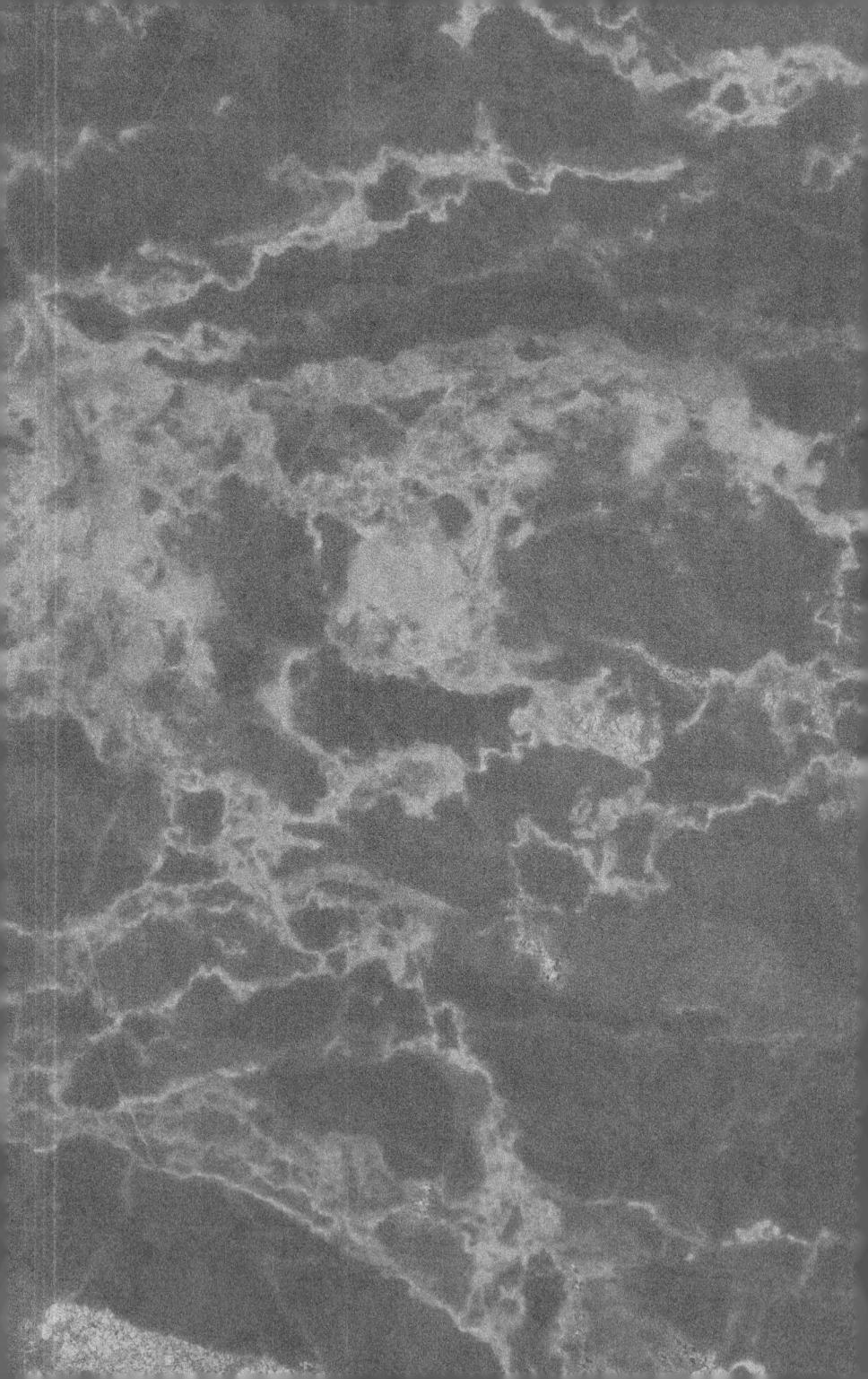

Obey

Obey By Lana Sky

Cover Design and Interior Formatting by Charity Chimni
Editing by Mickey Reed Editing
Proofreading by Charity Chimni

ACKNOWLEDGMENTS

Thanks so much to everyone who supported this draft along the way, including the many beta readers who provided encouragement along the way! Please keep in mind that this story includes dark, graphic and explicit content matter that is not suitable for readers under the age of 18—or for readers who are uncomfortable with the following subject matter: explicit sex, mentions of sexual abuse, mentions of child abuse, graphic depictions of violence, and mentions of self-harm.

CHAPTER ONE

I used to think I'd die before reaching twenty. Maybe I'd overdose on something? More realistically, I'd wind up stabbed to death by some shady-ass john.

Fairytales with shitty endings appeal more to me, anyway. The real Little Mermaid turned to dust in the end, and Snow White got buried in a glass box, all without getting the prince. I'm definitely not some fairytale princess—far from it, in fact. But maybe, just once, I want to know what it feels like. To dare to dream for something more than the inevitable unhappy ending. To want something so badly that you'd die for it.

After all, I've already killed for less.

"What are you thinking?"

The question rumbles against my eardrum. When I don't answer fast enough, warm lips part against the nape of my neck, releasing nipping teeth that demand obedience.

Answer me.

"S-something stupid," I croak, remembering where I am. Not a storybook setting, but a devil's lair. Black sheets conform to my exhausted form, soaking up sweat.

I risk looking over my shoulder from behind a fringe of my matted hair. A predator lies beside me, his skin glistening with sweat. Pale moonlight streams in through the window, casting him in a silver glow. If I squint and ignore the stench of salt in the air…

This moment could be normal pillow talk. How people in those shitty rom-com movies act after sex. Panting and still with limbs that almost touch.

One of those people wouldn't be bleeding though. They'd probably be closer in age, too. Not to mention, there wouldn't be a body in the foyer of their fancy high-rise—no, that would be a whole different genre. The kind in which the lead actor utilized a whip, left discarded somewhere on the floor.

"*Kotyonok.*" Maxim's tone snaps me back to the present. I've kept him waiting for a response for too long.

"Nothing," I say finally, licking my bitten, sore lips. "I'm thinking of a stupid game I used to play."

Or one my siblings and I used to, anyway. Proposing hypothetical wishing scenarios only poor brats could envision. Like: *Would you ever kill a man?* Or: *What would you do with a million dollars, Frankie?* For shits and giggles, we'd add a downside, just to make it harder to answer. *Hey,*

Frankie, what would you do if you committed murder with a man who had a million dollars?

Well...

I'd probably be in bed with said chiseled Adonis who seemed to own the whole fucking world. He'd have blond hair. Wild strands of it might fall across his forehead, casting a shadow over his piercing gaze. One look and my heart would clench as if jolted by a defibrillator. *Zap!* It's pathetic to admit, but only he would have that kind of power over me.

I'd let him have it.

Being so close to him would sting—worse than any bruise or cut I could ever inflict on myself. At least a knife would have a human impulse controlling it. Logic. Mercy.

But he wouldn't.

He'd be different. A beautiful, soulless contrast of ivory and shadow. All mine and yet so far out of reach. But, like the idiot I am, I'd forget that. Just for a second. I'd stare, eyeing the contours of his jaw in search of a hint of softness.

Maybe I'd find some, right *there* lurking within dark irises. I'd reach for it, my fingertips grazing flesh and muscle. Then he'd open his mouth and say...

"You slept." His voice resonates through my skin, his breath hot on my shoulder. "The first night I killed, I didn't."

I stiffen at the reminder, and then my hand falls to the sheets beneath us. Blood, violence, death. The memories circle my brain, forming a tornado of panic that almost drags me under—almost.

Like a good dealer, he already has another dose of my chosen poison on hand to keep me afloat. Rather than a bite or pinch, my antidote lurks in more violence, uttered like a bedtime story.

"I was a child then, the first time. My father would beat my mother, you see." His tone is so casual that he could be talking about the weather. Not death. "It was common among them," he adds. "His brothers. His father. It was even expected that I should hit her, should the feeling strike me to." He blows out a sigh that ruffles my hair. "But she was kind. Gentle. She barely raised her voice to him, and yet he would attack her just because the wind was blowing. There was no reason. No purpose. He just could."

His confession puts everything he's done to me in a newer context. The contracts. The safe words. Each layer is constructed to differentiate his preferences from those of an abusive prick. To prove to himself: *I'm not like him.*

Maybe it's enough of a difference. Or a lie. The same one I tell myself every damn day: I'm not like Melanie. I whore because I have to. I steal, cheat, lie, and fuck—all because I need to.

Like that makes it any better.

Like that makes it any easier to look at myself in a mirror.

"One night," Maxim continues, "he stormed into the house in a rage and struck her once. Just once, but she died instantly. Brain hemorrhage. Even as a child, I knew what he'd done. How little he cared in the aftermath—he kicked her when she didn't get up. Then he poured himself a scotch and headed up to bed, muttering how he'd make her pay in the morning. So I followed him." He remains silent for so long that I start to think he won't finish. Finally... "I don't even remember what I called him. He turned around and struck me across the face. In retaliation, I pushed him. He didn't die instantly, not like her. He was still alive, howling at the bottom of the stairs. He'd struck his head, but not hard enough to kill him. So I took a poker from the fireplace..."

Oh god. I squeeze my eyes shut as if the pathetic act can stop my brain from conjuring an image to match his tale. "Why are you telling me this?"

He sighs, breathing out harshly against my spine as I open my eyes again. "So that you will understand. Contracts aside, I am who I am. *This.*" He raises his hand, extending each finger as though his true nature is tattooed on each knuckle. "I will never hide this part of myself from you."

From someone else, I think the confession would sound romantic. Out of his mouth, it's a terrifying promise.

And he makes me chase it, staying silent until I ask, "What happened next?"

"I spent days in that house alone with their bodies. My grandfather was the one who found me. Found his son. I was afraid." No one would ever guess as much now. His voice lacks any true definition—just hoarse, emotionless words. "In my family, you can kill and abuse anyone *but* blood. The penalty is worse than death. But rather than punishment, he gave me my absolution: I was to head the division of the syndicate my father had. My family had a long heritage in running guns in and out of Russia, along with gambling. Overnight, I was given control of it all, with the same punishment my father faced should I fail: death. I was ten years old."

Heat prickles behind my eyes. Blinking doesn't push the tears back, and for the millionth time this week alone, I'm fucking crying. I can't stop it. In a way, I don't *want* to stop it. The moisture spilling down my cheeks tethers me to reality, far away from the twisted past he's reliving.

But not for long.

"I was weak," he says, continuing the thread of this fucked-up fairytale. "I still mourned my mother. Wept for her. And my grandfather was not pleased. To him, my actions were pathetic. He feared that I would never grow into a man. That I was too soft. Nothing should matter more to a man than his name. No *one* else. In his mind, he only saw one way to 'cure' me of those instincts."

His hand drifts down his torso to the edge of the binder shielding his stoma.

No. I'm holding my breath. My lungs are screaming for air, unable to take any in until he finally delivers the final piece of his story.

"He hired men," he says into my shoulder.

A sharp pain makes me jump: He bit me, giving us both a dose of the drug we've come to crave—but this time, it's not enough. I'm in the void with him, sucked into the past, forced to relive his horror to the very end.

"A group of them. To teach me why it would not be in my best interest to continue acting 'like a faggot,' as he put it."

Oh god.

I can't. I shake my head and then push him off. Away. In a rush of unfurling limbs, I try to crawl to the end of the bed, but he catches me, fisting his hand in my hair.

"I learned the truth about pleasure and pain that night, *kotyonok,*" he says in a chilling monotone. It's like once he's started talking, he can't stop. "You can never have one without the other, and I ensured that I would *never* be on the losing end again. I came to America. I built my own corner of our empire with my own fucking hands. I found people I could share it with."

He doesn't mean a family. Something more. I think of the British man, and Lucius, and the aura he's cultivated in his club. He built a new life.

"But *you.* I never planned for you."

Hot, searing pain splashes across my scalp as he yanks on my hair, drawing me into him.

"You are disgusted," he says, but he doesn't sound angry. Just resigned.

I crane my neck and find his mouth twisted into that terrifying emotion: confusion. His fingers trace my jaw as he studies my expression: my gaping mouth, my weeping eyes and what I know he finds in them.

Pity would be one thing, but this is different, unlike any agony he could ever dish out with a belt or his teeth. Something deeper than physical pain—it's understanding.

And it's fucking horrifying to feel it for someone like him. To feel it at all.

"I'm so sorry," I blurt as his frown deepens. "I'm so sorry—"

"Sorry?" Darkness clouds his gaze, and my heart sputters to a stop in my chest. When he reaches out, I'm frozen solid, but his fingers merely graze the length of my chin, tilting my face toward his. "One would think that, by now, you would stop surprising me, *kotyonok*," he says. Then he rolls toward his edge of the bed and stands. "I want you to answer this question honestly: Do you trust me?"

"W-what?"

"Trust," he snarls. "Do you know what it means?"

"I…"

I don't. Trust—that's a make-believe concept. I grew up being taught over and over that you only had one bitch on your side: the same one you saw in the mirror.

No one else was needed.

But him…

I know the word I want to say. I try to spit it out, but my brain scrambles it, turning the answer into something else. "I don't know."

Maxim nods. He's already dressed, and one of his hands dips into his pocket and withdraws a familiar object tucked into his palm: a knife. He flexes his wrist, springing the blade to its full length.

"My family thrives on 'trust,'" he says, mutilating the word like it's some sick inside joke. "On honor. Obedience. I am expected to follow any command given to me. No questions asked. No hesitation. Could I expect the same from you?" He takes a step in my direction, sending every muscle in my body into a frenzy. "The will to let me approach you with this blade and not so much as flinch because you trust whatever I will do with it. To you. Could you give me that?"

He smiles when I don't answer: a dangerous flash of teeth. "Stay here," he says, changing the subject. "I need to clean."

I swallow hard. Clean. In other words, remove the body. I can smell it from here, lingering beneath the musk of sex. Blood. Death…

"Get some rest, *kotyonok*."

When he leaves this time, there's no uncertain anticipation of what he might do next. I know: He'll come back.

And for whatever insane reason…I'll be here.

CHAPTER TWO

"Trusting" begins with a simple lesson, more basic than any so far. Wake up in his arms, breathing in his scent: a giant who holds me like a doll he doesn't want to break. Yet. The moment he senses I'm awake, his grip tightens, trapping me here. Beneath him. Beside him. Possession laces his touch, but it feels different from before.

My old collar was leather and gold, but this time...

Secrets bind me to him, forming a noose around my throat —one I'll never be able to remove. I can only endure it. Feel his skin molded against mine, sinew and muscle coiled with enough strength to kill. Take in everything Maxim Koslov has to offer...

And not flinch.

I last two seconds—the longest stretch I've ever gone with him. When I finally react, he pulls away and stands.

"Get up." After crossing over to a dresser, he removes a crisp white shirt and a pair of black slacks from it. "Up, *kotyonok*," he warns, frowning. I haven't moved. "As much as I'd love to punish your insolence—" His eyes rake over me and his tongue traces his bottom lip. Meeting my gaze, he sighs. "I'm taking you home."

Home. A part of me recoils even as I scramble upright. I can't imagine stepping foot back in the fucking shack again. The one place where I'm easy bait for Melanie the next time she comes knocking.

"Not there," he says as if reading my mind. "I'm taking you *home*."

The subtle inflection in his tone adds a terrifying new connotation to that word.

"What about my siblings?" It hits me that I don't have any idea where they are now. At the hotel? Somewhere else? My throat constricts. How could I have been so fucking selfish? "Where are they?"

"Safe," Maxim says. His tone paired with the knowing gleam in his gaze gives me an idea that he's handled it, taking all decisions right out of my hands.

Should I feel insulted? Petrified?

Still numb from last night, I can't decide. Absolution is a funny fucking thing in practice. It takes something more than the submission he craves—it takes desperation. I could fight back against his smooth insertion into my life or demand to know more.

Or I could say that fucking safe word and end it all now.

And he wants me to. That is why he's taking his time unfurling his shirt and pulling his pants on, waiting for the exact second I'll challenge him. When that moment never comes, he stands, fully dressed, his head cocked slightly to the side.

"Get dressed," he says and I lurch from the sheets and stagger to my feet.

He follows when I head toward my room, lurking in my wake. A glance down the hallway reveals that the center of the foyer is pristine, free of blood. Terror seeps in for a brief second, rooting me in place. My hand trembles, and for a moment, I let myself relive it.

The lack of resistance after the bone was crushed. The rusty smell of his blood painting my skin. The life draining from his eyes…what was left of them.

"*Kotyonok*." Maxim's hand lands on my shoulder, nudging me into the room down the hall from his. "Come."

With him in tow, I approach the closet and observe the clothing within. I don't even put up the pretense of choosing an item on my own. Sure enough, he reaches around me and flips through an array of hangers before settling on a black dress with a lacy collar. I start to pull it on, but he stops me, running his hand across my cheek.

"I need to wash you."

My stomach churns as I follow his gaze downward. My rust-colored hands reinforce a grim reality: I'm still covered in blood. So is he, though he doesn't seem bothered by the faint red streaks along his jaw.

In my bathroom, he guides me into the tub and washes me with his usual hyper-focused attention. My legs garner most of his care. He wrings the cloth directly over the worst of the cuts marring the pale skin—a savage array of lacerations on my inner thigh.

Reading the name they form over and over to myself doesn't make the ownership sink in.

Only when he roughly drags his thumb over an open wound do I feel the tug of that invisible chain.

You were made for me.

Once I'm finally dressed, he leads me to the front of the suite.

"I've had your belongings moved to a new location," he admits, confirming my suspicion: the home he referred to isn't the shitty two-story dwelling in Horn Hill that I've busted my ass all these years to protect.

Wherever he's taking me is a new realm. His.

My lips part, though I'm not sure why. Maybe I'll gather up the nerve to ask him more? Any words die in my throat as a buzzing tone draws his attention, and he withdraws a cell phone from his pocket.

"What?" he snarls, pressing the receiver near his ear. Whatever he hears from the other end makes his eyes dart in my direction, his jaw clenching. "No. I didn't know *he* was in town. Fuck—I'll be there." He shoves the phone into his pocket and heads for the sculpting room. "Go. Lucius will meet you out front. I'll join you later tonight."

It's funny. His tone is as cold and measured as always, but he's switched again, shedding any resemblance to the man who held me throughout the night. My brain processes his transformation in mockingly slow motion. How his eyes lose what little light they had. His mouth twists into that stern, haunting frown next. He's Mr. Hyde in the blink of an eye.

When I don't move, he jerks his chin toward the door. "I said go."

As expected, Lucius meets me in front of the building. Rather than head for Horn Hill or the hotel, his driver takes us to a townhouse in an upscale section of town, not too far from the high-rise. A block away, to be exact. It's a gated community right in the heart of Vermillion Heights—one of the most expensive sectors in the city. At first, I assume that Maxim wanted some other errand run first, but no. This is "home"—and it is way too much: an extravagant dollhouse fit for a toy.

"Here it is," Lucius announces as the car pulls into the driveway.

All I can do is stare. Overall, the house is made of stone, three stories tall, with old-fashioned fixtures. It's slightly beyond Maxim's sleek, modern style—more classic. It's beautiful. It's impossible. It's *borrowed*.

I tell myself that as I unbuckle my seat belt and step out of the car. When I see the house up close, my internal musing slips out. "He can't be serious."

"This way, miss," Lucius prods, as unshakably calm as always.

Shaking my head, I follow him up a path leading to the front door. Before Lucius can even knock, a beaming blond opens it and introduces herself as "Nancy," the new au pair. At my confused glance, Lucius shrugs—the most casual act I've seen from him yet.

"Mr. Koslov spared no expense in assuring that your family would be well taken care of," he explains.

What exactly that means remains to be seen.

The moment we step over the threshold, I hear screaming.

"Ainsley?" I rush toward the sound, but before panic can even set in, I register the scene unfolding in front of me: Ainsley and Eric are wrestling in the middle of a breathtakingly huge living room with a real fucking fireplace. The older kids are lounging on leather couches. When they see me, it's a stampede, and I'm suffocated beneath hugs and a million fucking questions.

"Frankie, what's going on?"

"What is this place?"

"Is this all ours?"

Rather than answer them, I shrug and force my lips into the shadow of a smile. "Can I have a tour?"

Ainsley takes charge to lead me through the house. It's huge. They each have their own bedroom, and I can't ignore the knowing shiver that runs down my spine once I see the décor of each one.

He knew—Maxim. He knew that Ainsley likes pink and Daisy prefers purple. He knew which room to supply with Teenage Mutant Ninja Turtles sheets and who to equip with an enormous dollhouse.

All of it feels too carefully catered to detail to seem accidental. No, he researched me. My life. My family.

And he chose a place Melanie will never be able to sneak her way into.

"Are you all right, miss?" Lucius asks once we return to the foyer.

"Yeah," I lie. My heart is racing, my palms slick. I'm not okay. Fear is a new kind of poison dripping through my veins. It doesn't make my thoughts feel any clearer. I'm just on edge.

As Maxim warned me himself, there was only ever one winner of the game.

So when is he going to finally pull the trigger?

All I can do is hope that the bullet comes before I get used to this. Before I get even more stupid—let my guard down any further.

I rarely pray, but here goes it: *Please, God, let him end this before this goes too far.*

Before I forget that this was only ever a game.

CHAPTER THREE

M axim doesn't arrive until after sunset, but the sound of him prowling across the foyer contrasts sharply with childish shrieks and bits of laughter drifting from the living room behind me.

I race to meet him, and my heart goes haywire as I watch him dominate the doorway. His shoulders are back, his posture neutral. If I didn't know any better, he could be a kind neighbor welcoming a new family into town.

Not the devil who owns me, body and soul.

"Stay," he says when I start for the door. "We're having dinner here tonight."

"W-what?" By the time I finally remember how to move, he's already halfway across the room. "Wait—"

"Who's at the door?" Ainsley demands, her cherub face peeking from around the doorway to the living room.

Oh god.

A suffocating pins-and-needles feeling comes over me as I observe Maxim towering over her tiny frame. When she spots him, she creeps to my side, her arms like iron bars around my waist.

"I'm a friend of your sister's," Maxim says, but there is a noticeable difference in how he responds to her versus me. For one, a warm smile unfolds over his mouth and his eyes lose a bit of their natural ice. When he sinks to one knee, I nearly jump out of my skin—but he only extends his hand, his expression one of pure charm. "I am very pleased to meet you."

Ainsley, who's painfully shy around strangers on a good day, manages to smile back. She even shakes his massive hand with one of her own.

Score one Maxim Koslov.

I watch awkwardly, unsure of what to do. "Should…should I give you a tour?" I ask as Maxim rises to his full height.

"No." Shaking his head, Maxim advances down the hall with an unnerving familiarity. "I'm sure dinner is ready."

"Dinner?" I ask, creeping in his wake, Ainsley in tow.

He must have called ahead. Planned this. The table in the dining room is already set for eight—by Nancy, I suspect. I hadn't even noticed.

After a whirlwind moment of introductions, I find myself shoved into a chair while all six kids take turns shouting over each other in a battle to narrate their week. What a difference a few fucking days of security can make. It's almost like we're a normal family for once.

There are no requests for new shoes or field trip dues. Just "I made a friend at the new school. Her name is Suzie."

"I actually passed a damn test."

"You look tired, Frankie. You look so tired…"

Alone, I'd have to fend the questions off by myself. Laugh on cue, smile, pretend. That was the price of security in the old days. I smothered my yawns of exhaustion and took one for the team. I sacrificed, even if it meant lying.

I'm not tired. The words are on my tongue, but for the first time ever, someone beats me to the punch.

"I am terribly sorry to have kept your sister away," Maxim says, his voice smooth and self-assured. "I've been keeping her busy these past few weeks."

Considering his sleek, black business shirt, red tie, and slacks, he resembles the type of man who might mean those words in the platonic sense only.

God, how appearances can be deceiving.

"She works for you?" The question comes from Mikie. His eyes are sharp, resembling how I guess I did whenever Melanie brought a new patsy around.

I don't know whether to panic or be proud. My heart is a swollen ball of nerves exploding in my chest.

LANA SKY

"Yes," Maxim replies without missing a beat. Seated beside me, he dominates this section of the table, dwarfing me and Daisy, who is sitting on the other side of him. Though his blond hair may be neatly slicked back and his hands free of blood, he's imposing.

I can't ignore the way the kids are mysteriously quieter around him, either. It's like they can sense what I would have in their place.

Nothing about this man broadcasts normal.

But, as if to prove me wrong, he shifts in his seat and his bulk suddenly seems less intimidating and more ungainly. The smile he's wearing helps. A little. To someone on the outside looking in, the expression might seem friendly. To me, it's a warning.

The scary part? I'm not sure of what. His glance in my direction conveys a silent message: *Relax.*

"Is it illegal?" Mikie demands, placing both hands flat against the table. Good boy. Stupid boy.

I try to meet his gaze. Shake my head. I'd be giving myself away, but what the fuck does stealth matter now? I know what happens when Maxim is pushed too far. The thought of him going at my brother with one of the polished steak knives from the table steals my breath away and my eyes dart to the door.

"Would your sister participate in anything illegal?" Maxim wonders.

22

His voice is neutral enough to draw a nervous laugh from the others, and the sound simultaneously drowns out my gasp as his hand settles over the small of my back. Thick fingers caress my spine, imparting a simple message: *I told you to relax.*

The room spins as a new voice joins the fray, announcing dinner. A maid? Whoever she is, she's smiling, but her pretty face drifts in and out of focus as she places a platter of food at the center of the table.

The kids attack in a blur of flying plates and silverware, and the chaos provides enough cover to disguise the warm lips that graze the side of my neck.

"Breathe. As I told you once before, I will not hurt them."

I didn't realize just how much I needed that reassurance. Some of the tension leaves my body in a sigh—some. Despite everything, one bastion of Maxim Koslov's character seems to hold true: He isn't a liar. At least, not intentionally—but any second the game could change.

Then again, believing him is the only shred of comfort I have to hold on to.

Dinner passes in a blur. Afterward, I juggle Ainsley on my lap, but I'm barely tethered to the warm, casual atmosphere everyone else seems to be feeling. My eyes don't leave Maxim once.

I'm hunting for the usual hallmarks of his anger: flashing eyes, clenched jaw. Instead, I find a new discovery that blows my mind. He keeps smiling, but it doesn't seem forced. He speaks when someone initiates a conversation with him—which, of course, is everyone, all at once. They flock to the relative newcomer, feeding off the novelty of a strange man who doesn't seem to be a criminal. Not outright, anyway.

They aren't up in arms like the way I've taught them to be around Melanie's conquests. I could write it off as just another part of Maxim's strange charm, but I know the truth. And it hurts.

They trust *me*.

And, what's even stranger, Maxim doesn't seem to forsake that. I can sense it in the way he keeps his posture open and relaxed even though such a stance doesn't come naturally to him. Neither does the small talk he endures.

"...and then I punched him," Ainsley says proudly, concluding her narration of one of her escapades on a playground. She eyes Maxim, her mouth wrinkled thoughtfully. "Have *you* ever punched someone?"

Maxim furrows his eyebrows as if seriously considering the question. Then he shrugs. "I prefer other methods," he says.

It's like being in the fucking Twilight Zone. I don't know how to react. So I just watch. I suffocate.

And, as if it's easier than breathing, Maxim Koslov effortlessly manipulates my family the same way he does me.

There's something seductive in the way he speaks when he's not growling out a command or a warning. His rich baritone caresses every word, making them ring out like musical notes.

I've never seen Daisy so relaxed around a stranger. He flatters Daisy with gentlemanly compliments, and he even gives Ainsley a "pony ride" around the living room when she demands it. He jokes with Mikie and the boys too.

I've never seen a man go out of his way to encourage this reaction in them and the shock of it all chokes me.

Torturing me aside, this is the most terrifying weapon that he's ever used. Pain is fleeting, but this? Normalcy is addictive—a drug I've never had. One that's too dangerous to ever indulge in.

"That's it. It's getting late," I blurt as the time creeps toward midnight.

When I finally usher the kids off to bed, it's like I can breathe again—and the instinct that took root the moment he arrived flares at full force. "You didn't have to do this."

"Do what?" Maxim doesn't miss a beat as he takes me by the arm and steers me toward the entryway, far from any listening ears—some of the kids must be watching from the stairs.

"This," I croak as the door closes behind us. I don't think air trickles into my lungs again until we've gone halfway down the front path. "I didn't... It's not good for them—"

"I didn't come here for *them*." He's dropped the charming act. All that's left behind is tension, which gnaws at the air between us. "This is what I can give *you*. More than pleasure. More than pain. More than sin."

I lick my lips, priming them to ask a dangerous question. "Like what?"

"More," he snaps. "Safety. Financial security. Support."

My brain instinctively shies away from those three words. I've never had them. Never needed them. Do I want them? I shake my head, my hair flying. Hell, I don't know if I'm trying to convince him or myself.

"Why?" I ask.

The contract, he should say—trading brutal sex for his money. Instead, he raises an eyebrow. "You can always tell me to leave."

It's a warning. I see his posture from the corner of my eye: broad, stiff, unmovable. His scent floods the air, filling my lungs. There is no escape.

Just surrender.

"Thank you," I croak. "But it's not good for them. Getting attached to someone. When this is over..."

"Ah." Maxim releases a low, rumbling chuckle that chills me to my very core. "You are still under the impression that this will be a temporary arrangement?"

"Isn't it?"

At least until the moment he gets bored, anyway. When he finds another woman to play with. Still, his words keep echoing in my head. *I will never let you go.* A part of me expects him to say them again. Reinforce it.

Never.

"Temporary," he says. A shadow flickers across his gaze as his fingers spread, gripping me tighter before releasing me. "If you say so."

He turns away, leaving me to follow him to the car. But while I walk, I can't shake the feeling that he laid down a trap.

And I stepped right into it.

CHAPTER FOUR

He makes me sleep in my room alone, but in the morning, his voice draws me awake.

"I need to wash you."

Later, when I'm dried and dressed, he enters the sculpting room and a terrifying thought sinks in. Despite everything, it is possible to forget what Maxim is. For five minutes maybe, when his shoulders aren't tense and his face is relaxed as he performs a hobby he obviously enjoys.

Something other than fucking.

But then, as if the universe has a vendetta against letting him appear human, something or someone quickly makes him raise his guard again.

This time, it's the door to the suite flying open and two men barging inside the studio. Make that *one* man, and he's dragging the other. I recognize the first's features before his voice rings out, tinged with a familiar accent. The British man from the club.

"I have a gift for you." He inclines his head at the man he's holding by the collar of a tattered sweatshirt. "My biker friend here may have some information that can help you with your…problem."

A scruffy beard obscures most of the blood streaming from what I think is the man's badly broken nose. One shove from the British man and he falls forward on his hands and knees. His dark, beady eyes flicker anxiously to Maxim. I wonder if he's from the same "biker" club as Melanie's last bastard.

"I know who you are," he says, spitting out blood. "You think you can kill me? The whole crew knows what you did to—"

"Good," Maxim says over him. "I didn't hide it. And unfortunately for you, I won't kill you. Yet." He sinks down low, still dangling a chisel from one hand. "First, I have a few questions I need to ask."

The biker goes three shades paler, but he bares his teeth, keeping up the tough act. "Like what, you motherfucker? We didn't fuck up your shit if that's what you're asking."

Maxim's eyes narrow and his hand flexes, tapping the edge of the chisel against the floor in a slow, lazy rhythm. "Oh? And you wouldn't happen to know who did, would you?"

The man chokes out a laugh and then grunts, clutching his nose. "And you don't?" he mumbles around his fingers.

"Funny, because the fucker is one of yours—"

"Go on," Maxim goads, his jaw clenching.

"Yeah. Blond guy. Same fucking accent as you. He your boy or something? From what I hear, he's been going around to everyone, ratting out your positions on everything."

Maxim goes rigid. He and the British man lock gazes and I get the sense that they're having a full-blown conversation without a word spoken between them.

"Him?" the British man asks, his tone hard.

Maxim says nothing. Before him, the thug grins, too smug to notice the alarming shift in his captor's posture. "Your warehouses," he sneers. "Where you do your runs. All that shit. I even heard that he's been asking about some bitch you fuck with by name." He nods in my direction. "This her? Francesca—"

"Go." Chisel in hand, Maxim is instantly transformed. His eyes darken, icy and flat. I can see my soul reflected in them as they gloss over my position in the corner. "Now, *kotyonok*," he tells me. The muscles in his forearms flex, a dangerous omen.

I start to move, but I only take a step before something in me falters. I stop. Maxim shoots me a glance, his eyes like midnight. There's a warning in them. A dare. *This is who I am.*

A monster.

Can you really accept me?

Seconds pass before my body makes the decision for me. I stay.

Turning from me, Maxim extends his arm, clenching his hands into fists. *Wham!* The violent thud of flesh striking flesh echoes like a gunshot, churning my stomach. In a sick arch, blood flies, painting a trail over the marble.

"Tell me more," Maxim demands as the man before him cowers, coughing up scarlet liquid. "Does he have a name, this 'fucker' of mine?"

The biker shakes his head. "I dunno," he croaks.

"Shame. Then I suppose our conversation has concluded."

Silver streaks the air and my mind takes a belated second to identify what it is: the chisel. *Thwack!*

It strikes skull. Bone. Flesh.

Again.

Again.

Again.

Maxim and his victim congeal into a shapeless blur of black and red as my eyes lose track of the violence. I can hear the noise. Taste blood.

Then it's over, and a harsh touch on my shoulder snaps me back to reality.

"When I tell you to leave, you leave."

I blink to find Maxim in front of me. His thumb shoots out, stroking my cheek. It's red, smelling of salt.

"Or do you think now that you've had a taste, you can handle this, *kotyonok*?" His eyes hone in on my quivering throat as I swallow to fight back bile. "You can't," he decides tonelessly. The chisel flies from his grasp as he turns away. "Go. And this time, do not make me tell you twice."

When he returns his focus to the helpless man on the floor, I dart into the hallway before the next blow lands with a sickening thud.

Then I run.

"You know it's him." The British man's voice chases me, a low, contemplating murmur. "Must our past keep haunting us because of your family?"

HOURS PASS before the whimpering finally dies off. From my position on my bed, I hear the front door open and then slam shut, which creates a chilling prelude to the slow, steady steps advancing on my room a second later.

He takes his time, turning my heartbeat into a rapid melody of surging blood and a hammering pulse. Just as it reaches a crescendo, my door opens.

These four white walls can't contain his bulk. They strain at the seams like an overstuffed birdcage and I'm the fucking canary. The half of my prison he dominates becomes a shadow, swallowed in darkness. My little corner contains the only hint of light seeping in through a nearby window, while my racing heartbeat floods the air. Only one of us can survive the impending collision.

Him?

Me?

What a stupid fucking question.

My knees knock together, but I can't move. I just wait. In a vain attempt to ground myself, my fingers flutter over my white duvet, cinching chunks of it.

"Look at me." One step brings him closer.

I smell him, choking on the scent of sweat and lust as my eyes adjust, seeking his shape out. His eyes glow, adding a chilling contrast to the bulge straining against the front of his pants. Instinct warns me that he's erect. Violence gets him off. So does fear.

So does *this*.

"You didn't run," he tells me, anger deepening the words into a guttural hum. "Not even when you saw the worst. You stayed. Do you think that makes you brave?"

I blink. The worst? He must mean torturing people in front of me, apparently—more than once.

But he's wrong.

The worst horrors he inflicts on me are what he's doing now: switching personas like hats. One man claims I was made for him. And the other? Made to spite him.

The only weapon I have in my arsenal is deflection. "Why did he say my name?"

He frowns, his head cocked. Just as quickly, he recovers, crossing over to the bed. With a well-placed swipe of his thumb against my lip, my body shivers, resonating with his possession. It's the strangest feeling imaginable—terror and need. It's like being on the edge of a high. Like bleeding out. Hemorrhaging.

"He was mistaken." His accent chops each word into several harsh syllables. "Forget him."

"What about that guy?" I croak. "The one I..." God, I can't even say the rest.

"Are you worried?" he counters. "Do you think I won't protect you?" He makes it sound so dangerous, doubting him.

A reply I can't swallow down springs to my lips. "What happens now?"

"Now..." He rolls his head along his shoulders, the closest I figure he can get to a casual shrug. "Have you consider what I asked you before?"

"What?"

"You can watch me beat a man to death...but can you give me your trust?" The way he speaks—strained and guttural —makes a part of me tremble. "Could you trust your life to me? No, I don't think you could." He shakes his head. "But the day you give me your trust—your full trust. There is nothing that I would deny you."

A dare? It's easier to focus on the mocking dip in his tone than the rest. His honesty is like a shotgun blast—lethal at point-blank range. I could test him like he said. Ask for something insane. Outrageous. Make him give me a response.

"So..." I swallow to clear my throat. "So, if I asked you for a million dollars—"

"You ask me for what you need. I will give it to you," he warns.

So, in other words, *yes*. If I needed a million dollars, he'd give it to me, in theory. The thought of that blows my mind.

He can't possibly mean it.

But the funny part is that, the longer I stare into his gaze, the more it seems like he does.

"So...how do I?" I croak. *Trust you.*

He comes to stand before me, his head cocked slightly to the side, those eyes fathomless. "Come here."

Holding my breath, I stand and approach him.

"Trust means nothing more than surrender," he explains. "I'm not asking for anything more than that. You. So get on your knees. Prove it to me."

On my knees. Prove it. He doesn't have to spell it out. My tongue slides along my lower lip, even as my instinct goes to war with logic.

Instinct wins: obey. I sink to my knees and shift toward him. He stays standing, though he spreads his legs wider when I reach for the fly of his slacks. With one tug on the zipper, his cock springs free. He's hard already. I can barely fit my lips around the swelling crown.

The moment my tongue cradles his shaft, I realize that this isn't like all the other times I've sucked him off. I hesitate for the space of a second, but he never grunts out any harsh commands. No orders to deepthroat. His hand grips my scalp instead, more for reinforcement than anything, driving the truth into my skull.

He's here. My goal is to pleasure him. Nothing else...

There are no dollar bills to mask my shame with. No salary to make it worth it. Just the slim knowledge that as long as I give him what he wants, he'll do the same.

Trust, I guess.

Slowly, I let my tongue drift up and down his length before spreading my lips around him again.

"Fuck," he grunts, the vibration rumbling through him.

With each suck, his grip tightens, pulling loose strands of hair. Ripping them *out*. It isn't long before he's pulsing at the entrance of my throat, demanding I take him in. All of him. Deep. Deeper...

For the second time, I have the same suspicion: Violence *must* turn him on. He's even thicker now. Straining. Some rabid impulse spurs me on, making me hollow my cheeks around him. I know he's at the edge when a burst of precum floods my tongue, ripe with his taste. Just when he starts to tense beneath me, his grip on my hair becomes a vise.

"Enough."

Before I can let him go, he drags me upright. My eyes flutter, taking in bits and pieces of the room—but he's already shoving me face down onto the mattress.

"Stay like this," he growls into my ear.

Drugged on anticipation, my brain struggles to interpret what he means. *Oh.* Like this: prone, at his mercy. *His.*

"Just like this…"

A sharp nip on my earlobe sends a jolt through me as his erection throbs against my inner thigh. Grasping, his hand travels down my hip to nudge my legs apart before guiding his length inside me.

One hard thrust and he's as deep as this position will allow. Fathomless. I can't even begin to silence my cry. So I don't, letting the sound ring out.

I squeeze my eyes shut, surrendering my body to the pace he sets. Fast. Slow. Slower. I come even before he spills himself inside me, and then I float back down to Earth just in time to feel the bed shift with his weight.

With his fingers in my hair, he tugs me toward him. Gnashing teeth meet my lips in a flurry, prying them apart, tearing me open. Kissing him always feels more penetrating than the sex. More intimate.

I'm breathing his air, inhaling his scent, and there is no boundary to negate the intensity.

He crushes me down, claiming my mouth with more ruthless need than he ever has my body. Harder. Deeper. I'm a writhing mass of sensation as muscle and bone react to his touch like a magnet. We're intertwined, skin on skin. Eager for more, I shift against him, sinking my fingers into his hair.

His words echo in my skull, a mocking taunt. *I can give you what you need.*

And maybe I want it: all of him.

Every inch.

Everything.

Something broken and unwarranted slips from my lips, mingling with his satisfied growl as his teeth nip at my jaw. "Maxim…"

Panting, he draws back, his gaze meeting mine, and my heart stops. He's beautiful like this. He's terrifying like this —because he's too close. My thoughts scatter and I almost forget the truth of why I'm here. Why he's kept me with him.

Necessity.

This is just a game, but I can't stop myself from dragging my fingers along the planes of his face anyway, adding more bullets to the barrel of this dangerous round of roulette. There's no pain in this moment to get me high. No thoughts of money in my head. Just him. And he's enough. I'm not just a desperate hooker anymore.

"Maxim—"

"No!" Suddenly, he wrenches back as if electrocuted. Within seconds, he's at the other end of the room. His chest heaves, muscle rippling with every breath he takes.

Our gazes reconnect and my blood runs cold at what I find in his: nothing. Not lust. Not hate.

Just shadow, dark enough to paralyze me despite the haze of sex weighing me down like a cloud.

His lips twitch, preparing to say something.

But, without a word, he turns and leaves, slamming the door in his wake.

My heart won't stop pounding and sweat pours off my skin, dampening the sheets beneath me. The man is bipolar—I know that.

Even so…I did this.

Someway, somehow, I crossed a line.

And I know he'll punish me for it.

CHAPTER FIVE

I wake up alone. Without Maxim.

Without anyone.

When the sunlight starts to stream in through the windows, I get dressed, picking out a simple gray dress that seems like the safest choice. For what feels like hours, I sit on my bed, waiting. The second I hear the door to the suite finally open, I'm on my feet, creeping into the foyer—but rather than Maxim, I find Lucius waiting for me.

"Mr. Koslov thought you'd enjoy spending time with your family today," he says, smiling.

It's funny. I've almost forgotten what it feels like: spending time with them.

When I finally reach the house, they're sprawled over the living room, spilling snacks all over the floor—crumbs that Ainsley promptly grinds into the floor as she rushes to greet me.

"You're back!"

Back. Like I was away long enough for my absence to be noticed. But maybe I was…

Ollie and Ray clear a space for me on the couch while Daisy and Mikie launch into descriptions of their new school, and the reminder cuts into my psyche like a lance. Maxim.

All of this is possible only because of him.

They're safe, only because of him…

Hours later, Ainsley's in the middle of reading me a story when Lucius receives a phone call. One look at the screen and he chooses to answer it in the hallway—but even from the living room, I catch snippets of his conversation.

"What? So soon?" He sounds startled, and he lowers his tone. "No. You shouldn't go alone, but I will go with you. Sir, I—you know that these matters are private. Delicate. No, I'm not questioning you, sir. I… Are you sure?"

He repeats that last phrase at least three times. *Are you sure?*

To Lucius' credit, he's smiling when he appears in the doorway and motions for me—but it's one of those strained smiles typically worn by a used-car salesman who knows that the old Buick he's trying to sell you might blow up if you take it for a test drive.

"Mr. Koslov requests your presence," he says, leading the way to the door.

During the ride over to the suite, he says nothing. Though, when I finally climb out of the car, I find him watching me through the windshield. He's frowning, his mouth taut, and recognition runs down my spine as I trip onto the curb. It's an expression I've seen only once before: after Maxim beat a man to death in front of an entire roomful of people.

That helpless, resigned sort of look. "Goodbye, Ms. Marconi."

My stomach is in knots when I stagger into the building, but I try to shake the feeling off as I head up to the suite. A minute later, the elevator doors part to reveal a figure pacing in the hallway.

Maxim snarls, each syllable reverberating like thunder. "Do you think *you* can dictate to *me*?"

Instinct overrides everything else. I stagger back, but before I can choke out a pathetic defense, I notice the cell phone pressed against his ear. He's dressed casually—another warning sign. On second thought, maybe the look is more ironic than anything. The black shirt and slacks help him cut an imposing silhouette against the wall and accentuate his blank, hard expression: a fallen angel in limbo.

"I'm not a dog," he growls into the speaker of the phone, directing the venom at whoever is on the other end. "*No one* calls me to heel. Tell him that I will come in my own time." In a violent motion, he winds his arm up like a baseball pitcher and hurls the phone. A second later, it shatters against the wall. "*You.*" His gaze hones in on me, trapping me against wood and metal.

I swallow hard, rocking onto my heels. There are so many things about this man that I'm beginning to understand. Like when he's furious. Or when he's uneasy. Surprise, surprise, *both* emotions waft from him now. Which one is more dangerous?

Who the fuck knows.

"Come." Without another word, he heads for the private stairwell rather than the elevator. One of his hands wrenches the door open so hard that it slams against the wall, which startles out the breath I didn't even realize I was holding. "I said come."

My fingers rush to smooth the skirt of my dress as I follow him down to the bottom level: the garage. Rather than approach his own car, Maxim leads me out to the front of the building, where Lucius' driver has pulled another vehicle around. Without hesitation, Maxim claims the back seat, motioning for me to as well.

"Sir?" the driver asks once the door closes behind us.

Minutes tick by before Maxim answers. He sprawls out over his end of the seat, glaring at the nearby buildings and streets the same way he eyes his battered blocks of stone, chisel in hand. That cold frown tugs on his lower lip; it's the one he typically displays when he's looking for a weak spot to pummel into submission.

"The house in Black Briar," he says before the suspicion can finish unfurling in my mind. His eyes flashing, he rests his head back against the seat, radiating exhaustion and annoyance in one swift motion. "You know the one."

"Yes, sir." The driver nods, and not even ten minutes later, we arrive before an imposing brownstone—this one in an even more exclusive part of the city, secluded behind an iron gate.

From the front of it alone, I can't tell what sort of person might live here. Just that they value their privacy. *A lot,* judging by the men lurking around the edges of the estate. They eye the car warily, their hands on their pockets.

If I thought Maxim might explain why we're here, I was wrong. He simply observes the property before finally climbing out of the car. One of his hands snatches my wrist, pulling me after him.

"Come."

It's a short trip up a narrow stone walkway to reach the front door. Maxim knocks once. Not even a second later, a woman wearing a black uniform opens the door. Her graying hair neatly tied back into a bun.

"Mr. Koslov." She bows her head in respect and then scurries deeper into the house. A whispered statement floats back to us, uttered cautiously. "He's expecting you."

Maxim's shoulders stiffen as he pulls me along, rippling with tension not even his cold, expressionless mask can hide.

I can barely see my hand in front of my face—it's *that* dark in here. It's as if the person who designed this place wanted to make sure that, even on a sunny day, very little light would reach the interior. Dark walls and polished wood create a harsh contrast between light and shadow. Very few items of furniture or decoration add any definition to the rooms we pass, either. Just winding hallways that make each footstep echo for what seems like miles.

Finally, the woman, who I assume is a maid, stops near a doorway and then darts away. I catch only a glimpse of the room from over Maxim's shoulder before he drags me inside.

It looks like a study. Shelves of leather-bound books frame an open space where a man is sitting behind a mahogany desk. He's handsome in a harsh way, with stark features framed by blond hair, streaked with gray. Like Maxim, he's wearing black: a tailored suit with flashing silver cufflinks.

He spares one look in our direction and it suddenly feels colder here than it did outside.

"Maximov..." His voice is raspy, distorted by a heavy accent. "I was wondering when you would finally scurry before me." He extends his right hand, displaying a silver ring on his thumb.

Maxim says nothing. Does nothing. Frozen in place, he stands at the mouth of the room, still holding me by my wrist. There's no life in his touch. I might as well be held by a goddamn statue. Looking at his face, I can't discern anything from his gaze. Not anger. Not even fear.

He's soulless.

An icy dread washes over me. It is the same feeling I got when he nearly beat me to death with a belt. And when he spilled the dark secrets of his childhood. Like he's not really here but far away, reliving a horror no one else can see.

"Did you hear me?" The man raises his hand again, reaching out over the surface of the desk this time. Two of his fingers flicker in a silent command. "Show some respect, *mal'chik*."

That name cuts through Maxim like a knife. One ragged inhale and he's alive again. In one smooth motion, he crosses over to the desk, but his grip on me doesn't let up and he hauls me forward as well. Once he's close enough, he lowers his head in order to brush the surface of the ring with his lips.

"Grandfather," he grates out before returning to his full height.

Terror smothers my shock. His grandfather. The one responsible for his stoma.

Anatoli.

Does he hate this man? When the two finally lock gazes, I can't tell. Maxim seems farther away than ever.

Chilled and distant, his voice rings out. "You called for me?"

Anatoli scoffs. "Men are *called*. But boys?" He rises to his feet and has to stoop to keep his head from brushing the edge of a hanging chandelier—he's *that* tall. "Boys are whipped into submission." There's an unexpected grace in the way he moves from behind the desk and advances on our position.

With every step he takes, the tension coiled in Maxim's grip gets tighter...tighter... Like a fucking powder keg ready to blow. When the man places a hand on his shoulder, the pressure on my wrist intensifies. Fuck, I swear for a second that he might break it.

"It's been a long time," the man says softly. "But your current results have disappointed me. Perhaps you need another lesson on how to be a man, *mal'chik*?"

Maxim's entire body vibrates. His grip becomes iron, his nails piercing my skin. I can't swallow my gasp—and then Anatoli finally seems to notice me here.

"You brought a toy." The disapproving tone cuts through me, but just as quickly, he returns his attention to his grandson. "After all this time, one might think you'd learned your lesson. Are you aiming to insult me?"

The question strikes like a knife. To bear the impact, Maxim grits his teeth, his expression blank.

"Or maybe she's a toy for Sevastyn?" Anatoli wonders. "A thank-you for cleaning up your mess."

For a brief second, shock disrupts Maxim's hardened mask. "Sevastyn?" he says, grating the name between his teeth. "You requested an audience with *me*—"

"Don't play the fool, Maxi." The voice comes from a man who appears in the doorway, and I have to blink just to dispel a sense of déjà vu. With long, wild, blond hair and dark eyes, he is Maxim's twin—just as massive and just as intimidating. His face is thinner though, bonier, and where Maxim scowls, he smiles. "Don't pretend that you don't know what this is about." He runs a hand along his black suit, flicking away invisible dust. "Or perhaps the rumors are true? All these years have made you soft."

"Grandfather," Maxim says, focusing solely on the man near the desk. "If you want to discuss business, you speak to me. In private—"

"Oh?" Sevastyn chuckles. "And what *should* be private, Maximov? The mess you've made within the past month? Or the punishment that awaits should you fail? Again?" His lips pull back from yellowed teeth as he flicks his thumb along the stubble on his chin. "Perhaps my father is right and a lesson may be in order? I still remember a trick or two to bring you to heel—and you certainly need reminding of your place. Rumors have spread. That you've made an enemy you shouldn't have."

"I have the right to defend my interests," Maxim says coldly.

"Do you?" Anatoli waves his hand dismissively. "Or are you too busy settling personal scores? Send your toy away. Now."

Maxim steps forward, nudging me behind him. "Go."

I don't think twice before escaping into the hall. The door closes behind me, but my ears pick up noise they shouldn't: low murmurs dominated by a raspy growl I know to be Maxim's. Most of the conversation is too distorted to make out—Russian, I think—but I can tell from the insistent tone that it's an argument. A heated one.

When the door finally opens again, Maxim looms behind it, leaning against the doorway as if for support. His lack of stability isn't what sends my pulse racing, however. It's his eyes; they're fixed ahead of him, hollow and black. Dead.

Behind him strolls Sevastyn, his teeth bared. "I hope you understand, dear nephew," he says, placing his hand on Maxim's shoulder. "Blood may be blood, but business is business. Though I'm not averse to mixing it with pleasure." His gaze cuts to me. "Is this one of the morsels from your club? A bit scrawny—"

"She's no one," Maxim replies in haltingly clear English. "And I do *understand*. But"—a shadow flickers over his face and he stares down at his shoulder and violently shrugs off the hand on it—"Anatoli or not, you touch me again and *I will kill you.*"

"Is that so?" A mocking laugh chases him over the threshold. "Next time, leave your toys at home, *mal'chik*. Perhaps then you can face me like a man."

When Maxim's gaze finally focuses on me, I tremble. From head to fucking toe. The instinct to run is almost too strong to swallow down, rising up the back of my throat. My legs twitch, my knees knocking together. His expression…

I only saw him like this one other time.

That very first day when, to him, I was nothing more than a nameless whore.

Replaceable.

But I'm not. The pathetic assurance comes from some distant, naive part of my brain as he steps past me and advances down the hallway. His hand shoots out, snatching me forward. Like iron, his grip dominates my wrist, radiating possession and I can breathe again. I'm the only one he's kept.

The only one to stay.

Despite the contract.

Despite everything.

CHAPTER SIX

He takes me back to his suite. Without a word spoken, he storms into his sculpting room and I linger in the foyer for hours, listening to him work. Hammer. Pound.

Destroy.

Only God knows what set him off this time. Eventually, he calls to me, his voice a rasp. "Come here."

I step toward him, fighting to keep my fear from showing on my face. Then I fail. My bottom lip trembles, and the corner of his mouth flicks down in response: a dangerous frown.

"Do you know what you saw today?"

It takes me three tries to suck in enough air to reply. "No."

"Of course not." His eyes lose their hungry gleam as that beautiful mouth straightens into a cold, lethal line. It's only now that I realize he's covered in dust. The grayish sheen makes him look frozen in the cold air around us. "My organization was nearly ripped from my fucking hands. *My business.*" He stares down at his fingers, flexing them in and out of fists. "Everything I've worked for. Why?"

He lets the question hang in the air, but in the end, he comes up with his own answer.

"Maybe I've been distracted…"

It's dark in this room, but the glow from the sculpture area gives definition to his body, highlighting the sweat and signs of exertion I didn't notice before. His hair is damp, his body rippling with tension.

"Look at me."

I don't even notice him move until it's too late. Upon grabbing my chin, he wrenches it back so that I have no choice but to meet his gaze again. His fingers creep down to my throat, tightening. Squeezing.

Choking.

This isn't a sexual game. His eyes don't hold a shred of warmth or lust. Just ice.

Alarmed, I use my hands to claw at his grip. "M-Max—"

"I could kill you," he says, dangerously soft. "I could. Maybe I should?" His grip tightens to cut off my windpipe entirely. "Before they do it for me."

I wheeze as my pulse surges in a futile rhythm. He's holding too tight. Too long. Just as spots speckle my vision...

He shoves me back.

Weightless, I crash into the leather chaise on the other side of the room. Air wheezes in and out of my chest as my eyes burn and overflow. My throat is on fire. For what feels like an eternity, I can't stop gagging until I bring up bile that coats the floor. When I finally get my bearings, he's gone, slamming the door behind him.

And I'm left alone in hell.

Around me is a mess of disheveled pillows. A lamp was knocked over and is in pieces on the floor. The chaise is askew.

Unease twists my stomach into knots and I have to curl up on my side as I process what happened. Something tells me, even before I reach up to feel the tender skin along my throat, that his grip will leave a mark.

"I could kill you," he said.

How close did he come to doing just that?

You don't want to know, a part of me warns as more burning tears spill down my cheeks. *You don't fucking want to know.*

WE HAD a cat a few years ago. Some stray Daisy had let in and Ainsley had enough heart to name. Whiskers, or something like that, I think. Something stupid. Forgettable. I only let her stay around for as long as she did because she'd go after the mice or roaches every now and again.

I saw her trap one once. For the longest time, she watched it scuttle around, just out of her reach, before swiping at it with her paw—but she didn't kill it. Not right then. For what seemed like hours, she wounded it bit by bit, letting the poor thing get just far enough away to tease escape before capturing it again.

It was only when it gave up the fight that she put the poor bastard out of its misery. Sometimes she didn't even eat it. The game was enough to fulfill her—until it wasn't. Boredom was her prey's final sin, and only then would it face the ultimate punishment.

It's funny how those warning signs witnessed in a wild alley cat can translate over to a much larger beast. A monster with black eyes, golden hair, and maybe half the patience of old Whiskers. A part of me knows the awful truth, even before his fingers roughly graze my inner thigh, jolting me awake.

"Look at me."

He's empty when I do, but it's not like any other time before. Except maybe that first day I met him in his suite... Once again, I'm just a hole, used up without an acknowledgment or foreplay. He sinks into me roughly, grinding my body into the mattress.

His hand grips the back of my throat throughout, like a noose capable of cinching off my windpipe at any moment.

He's testing me. No, it's worse than that. He's testing himself. I can almost trace the twisted trail his mind wanders in the resounding quiet. Fear rides my spine, paralyzing me on sweat-soaked sheets.

But I'm too fucking chicken to run.

How dangerous this man is when he *thinks*. When he broods. He mulls over his thoughts the way an assassin polishes his weapons. Slowly. Carefully. He can't let so much as a sliver of metal lose its lethal edge.

So he becomes obsessive in his meticulous routine, wielding sanity like a switchblade.

Flicking it on.

Off.

On.

Night brings out the worst in him, but I'm realizing I fear the day more. It's the quiet after the storm with no shadows to disguise the damage left behind.

I'm dreading the moment I have to peel my eyes open again, despite the fact that I never slept. Not really. My stomach aches with the threat consciousness brings: clarity. I bury my face into the pillow beneath me, hoping to linger in oblivion for a few seconds longer.

Too late.

His heavy sigh shreds the oppressive silence. Then he stands, still gloriously naked. Uneasy, I watch him, slack-jawed from over the crook of my elbow. The moment his feet hit the floor, he's untouchable, miles away from me in a world where I don't exist.

He takes his time reassembling the cold exterior I've come to associate him with. His shirt goes on first, and he buttons it the whole way up. The pants are next. Dark eyes gazing at me from behind a fridge of wild hair are the last detail he arranges. They narrow, hardening like winter ice. He heads for the door—but the final look he casts my way might as well be directed at the wall.

And then I know.

Maxim.

Is.

Bored.

He's a lot less subtle than my cat. He never pretends that escape is an option. If anything, his suite becomes my prison even as he spends most of the time somewhere else. His brief absences become hours. Then days at a time.

By the end of the week, I'm not his *kotyonok*. I'm not even Francesca. I'm just a slave, beckoned by snapping fingers and the unzipping of his fly. Those brutal, violent fucks become snatches of oral sex.

Until one night...

He doesn't return to the suite alone.

I smell her first: cheap perfume like the kind Melanie wears. Just enough to hide the scent of sex from other men, but not enough to cloak her desperation. Stumbling in Maxim's shadow, she's skinny, wearing cheap high heels and a low-cut dress in a tacky zebra print. A long, tangled wig obscures most of her naturally brown hair, framing a face that's almost pretty. Her eyes widen when she sees me standing at the mouth of the foyer.

"Double-team is gonna be extra," she slurs, her voice high-pitched and breathy.

I'd peg her age at a year older than I am. Maybe even two. She's been around the block more than once. Still, there is something unnerving in her smeared lipstick and unfocused, brown eyes. The desperation reeking from her in waves feels familiar. She even *looks* familiar. Like me with a bad dye job, viewed through a blurred mirror. A more broken, more fucked-up Francesca.

Without a word, Maxim steers her to the leather chaise in the center of the main room. He sits, and she stands, trying to look sexy while he palms her tiny waist in his hands and hikes her dress up to her hips. Her bare ass is sporting a handprint—some john wasn't very nice. I wonder if that's why she's consented to let someone like Maxim take her back to his private suite. How desperate is she? How much money does she need?

What has he promised her?

Or maybe she's not doing it for the money at all. Her moan is real as Maxim drags her closer, his head lowering toward her waist. Whatever he does makes her sway on her feet, her back bow...

"What are you doing?" I don't even sound like myself. That soft, weak whisper could never come out of the Francesca Marconi I knew.

"Get out." Maxim doesn't even look at me. "I said get out!" There's no mercy contained within the syllables. No lust. Just a command: *Go.*

I try. I *do*, taking a step toward the hall. My vision blurs. The hooker becomes a multicolored smear as her moan deepens, and the room starts spinning.

As if from far away, a woman gasps while a man growls, his anger rippling to the farthest corners of the room like thunder. I'm transfixed by my shadow, how it sways back and forth. Back and forth.

"Did you hear me?" He's practically snarling.

Maybe it's pathetic, but my mind searches desperately for an explanation. Shaking, I blurt out the first one I can come up with. "Is this because of what that man said?" His creepy, blond doppelganger Sevastyn. His attention still burns, making my skin crawl. "That I'm—"

"Stop." He shoves the girl aside so hard that she trips into the wall, not that he spares her a passing glance. Like honed missiles, his gaze seeks out mine, ripping through me. "You think you can even question me?"

"I thought you wanted..." I can't even say it out loud. *Trust.*

"What I want?" He stands and advances on my position while fastening his slacks. "I *want* you to learn your place." He lunges, grabbing my arm.

Before I can react, he turns and marches to the door, dragging me from the suite and into the stairwell. My heart hammers as I stagger down the steps after him, forced into the garage. When we reach the car, he heads straight for the passenger's side and shoves me in before claiming the driver's seat for himself.

The moment he closes the door behind him, Maxim takes off, plunging headlong into the thick of traffic. He's reckless, as if the speed limit is nothing more than a design tacked onto the signs we pass.

He heads deeper into the heart of the city. Far beyond the bars and strip clubs and into the land of icy business and jaw-dropping wealth—all unfamiliar territory to someone like me. This paranoid part of me can't help thinking the destination is on purpose: *Even if you manage to run, you won't get very far...*

I swallow the fear back and put all of my effort into trying to decipher our surroundings. Gray skyscrapers tower above, blocking out what little remains of the overcast sky. Suddenly, the car turns and the interior plunges into darkness before I can make out what exactly he entered. A parking garage? The place appears to be a single level, devoid of any other cars.

"Come." He parks and climbs out, leaving me to follow him through the metal fire exit that opens onto a narrow hallway.

The air tastes like rust here, and I find myself shivering as he leads me through a maze of corridors and finally into a large, open room I don't recognize.

The walls are black. The floor is bare cement, and in the center of it, someone spread out a large square of plastic tarp. Not just any quality, either—it's the kind butchers use when they cut up an animal. I know only because Melanie dated one once upon a time. The back of his shop resembled this room in a way: cold and semi-dark. The only difference is that, instead of carcasses of cows, hunks of stone in various stages of sculpting linger around the corners.

"Strip," Maxim tells me as my eyes blink rapidly to adjust.

Confusion weighs my veins down like lead; I'm too slow. It feels like an eternity before I finally manage to bend and remove my shoes first. Then my dress. Panties. Bra. When I'm naked, Maxim leaves my clothes untouched and jerks his chin toward the tarp.

"Lie on it."

I'm allowed only two seconds to comply on my own before he grabs me by the shoulder and drags me closer to the edge of the tarp himself. One shove and I go down hard, landing on my side, tasting blood. I must have bitten my cheek.

True terror creeps beneath my skin as I watch him through a jagged fringe of my hair. With an almost beautiful elegance, he heads for a corner of the room, where tools hang from the wall. They're sharp, glinting in the dim lighting. After a moment's observation, he grabs one seemingly at random—but it just so happens to be the sharpest: a knife. When he turns to face me again, my entire body tenses up in recognition.

I *know* that look.

"Face the wall," he commands, his voice strained and gritted. His boots thud against the floor as he advances step by goddamn step. His shadow dances over the floor behind him, beautiful broken wings. "Now."

Choking a question down, I obey, facing the darkness. The only light comes from a naked bulb dangling from a chain in the ceiling. Even so, I can still make out his silhouette— every thick, brutal limb. Every ounce of lean muscle. Looming over me. Swallowing me.

"On your knees." His footsteps trail off a few feet away.

My ears pick up a noise my brain races to identify: something moving through the air. Cutting through it. I flinch before I feel the burning sting between my shoulder blades.

"Ah!" My gasp slips out despite how I bite my lip to seal it back. Already, something warm drips down my lower back, pooling at my waist. God, I can feel it.

Drip.

Drop.

"I said *on your knees.*"

Another rush of air ruffles my hair, but I still don't expect the second blow. It catches me across my hip, biting deeper than the first. Another cry escapes my throat, and a second later, I hear a metallic cling as if something struck the floor. From the corner of my eye, I catch the knife rolling into a corner. The brief moment of distraction costs me: Maxim lunges. One firm nudge against my ass—his foot—and I lurch onto my hands and knees, slamming my forehead on the floor.

"Now..." He breathes heavily as pain shoots through my skull. "Open your mouth."

He circles around me, wrenching at the fastenings of his pants. His jaw is clenched, his eyes shielded by his wild hair. He pulls twice on his fly, and I brace myself when he finally frees his cock. Like always, he's breathtaking—but this time for an entirely different reason.

Nestled in that thatch of golden hair, he's not hard. I blink to make sure. Again. Nothing changes before the pressure on my hair tightens. He yanks my head back, forcing me to meet his gaze. The crazed expression I find is nothing like the cold Maxim I know. I don't think he even fucking sees me.

"I told you to open your goddamn mouth." He drags me forward, forcing his limp cock against my parting lips.

I try to obey, take him in, but...it doesn't feel right. He cringes from the contact, even as he pulls me against him, shoving his length deeper into my mouth. My tongue reacts instinctively to cradle him, and vibrations run through my teeth—he's shaking.

When I try to suck, he shoves me away.

"Fuck!"

The shout rings out as I fall back, hitting my head on the floor. Stars dance before my eyes, obscuring the figure hovering above me. Or maybe it's the tears? I still see the shape of his arm move though. It whistles through the air like a missile a heartbeat before the bitter sting sears through my cheek. *Wham!*

Shock renders me paralyzed. Pause. Rewind. Play.

He hit me.

My brain barely registers the blow before his fingers are in my hair again, tugging, pulling. He grabs my hand in one of his, forcing me to grip his cock. A growl rips from him at the contact, but it's not out of pleasure. His hips buck away from me. His fingers tremble, struggling to maintain their grip. When he attempts to make me stroke him, he lurches back on the balls of his feet, knocking me away again.

"Stop! *Do not touch me.*"

I blink, staring up at him as every ounce of air in my lungs shrivels into nothing. His eyes are wild. Haunted. Insane. They drift over my body and find the knife again. He steps toward it and I know that this time...

This time, just drawing blood won't be enough. My screams won't be enough.

God, I know that look. It's hatred, violent and unrestrained. It's the way I look whenever I think about Melanie. It's loathing. It's pain.

My lips flutter apart. I mean to say the safe word. I try to choke it out—but different words spill from my tongue instead.

"You hit me." I sound so goddamn pathetic. So fucking surprised. A man who pays me for violent sex hit me when he felt like it. So hard that I bit my tongue. So hard that I saw black. So damn hard. "You hit me."

He blinks, caught off guard, and staggers back a step, staring around the room as if seeing it for the first time. Then his eyes return to me, resigned. "So what if I did? You are a whore. *Suka.* I give you money, you do anything. Do you really think you mean more than that?"

Do I? Did I?

My head is an endless rush of a million different thoughts. It hurts. The world isn't spinning anymore—the merry-go-round is in fucking flames.

He's not the first man who's hit me. He won't be the last.

But he's the only one—*no.* I dig my nails into my palms to cut the thought off, but it's too late. Too painful. Too pathetic.

He's the only one I didn't expect it from. Not like this.

"I'm…" I suck in air, struggling to choke the words out. Just two. "I'm—"

"Happy?" he finishes for me. "You think that will be enough? That it will be *that* easy?" He laughs, throwing his head back with every broken chuckle. "You think I really give that much of a damn about some stupid little bitch? I will kill you, and do you want to know what I will do after that? I pay off the police. I dump your body. At most, it will cost me a day. Nothing less. Nothing more."

He's still laughing as he says it. It's the truth. Knowing that churns my stomach. It cuts me into pieces. And I wish it were because of fear. I'd give anything to scream. To run. To say that fucking safe word.

I'm in his head again—and I know why he brought me here: the sick, violent reasons. I know what he wants to prove to himself. Like the night when Melanie left again, Daisy was sick, and Ainsley was a baby. When *I* was a fucking baby. I didn't know what to do. How to cope.

So I turned my pain on the only fucking person who deserved it. I took a knife from the kitchen sink. I cut myself deeper than I ever have. More than I ever have. I lost so much blood. I even lost consciousness.

The only thing that saved my life was that I didn't nick an artery.

And even after all that, the next morning, all I could do was wrap an old pair of stockings around my wounds and get the kids ready for school. I kept going. Kept living.

Maxim Koslov isn't living. He's playing with the edge of the knife, toying with how deeply to cut himself this time. How much of a mess can he make before it all becomes too much? Game over.

Whatever happened within the past few days snapped something inside him. He'll kill me now. I know it.

But I can't run. So I wait, letting those black eyes stare dead into my own. With every second that passes, they grow brighter. Crazed. Maddening.

It's like looking into a goddamn mirror.

"Do not..." His voice shakes as if he's struggling to maintain control. "Do not think that I will not hurt you, *kotyonok*." He lashes out, grabbing my throat before I can react. Gradually, his grip begins to tighten, cutting off my windpipe. "Because I will. Make no mistake about that." More pressure is added to prove his point. "Weakness is always exploited. Never forget that. Before you could ever be used against me, I would eliminate you myself."

As soon as I begin to sputter under the pressure, his hand jerks free and I'm left panting, trying to grasp what the hell just happened.

Weakness. The word reverberates through my mind. *Weakness.* His own words break loose from the tangled mess of my thoughts. *To teach me. I was too soft. He hired men...*

"Your family..." I choke out on another gasp of air as more twisted puzzle pieces fall into place. That distant look in his eye. The way he reacted when I mentioned his uncle. The violence now. "You think they will hurt me."

Maxim goes rigid. His arms fall flat at his sides, his eyes wide like I slapped him this time. Two steps backward carry his body into the wall and the blow resonates throughout the entire damn room. Slowly, he sinks into a crouch, his back braced against the wall. His voice cracking, he commands, "Get out."

But I can't fucking stop.

"They hurt you before—" Horror robs me of my voice. I just whisper, dragging my gaze down to his hip. *Oh god.* His pain seeps into me and everything feels too clear. I picture the way he reacted when that man—his uncle—touched him, and my stomach starts to crawl up the back of my throat. "Did he do that to you? Your uncle—"

"*Leave!*"

I should. My limbs unfurl as blood sticks the tarp to me. When I finally gather up the strength to rise on my hands and knees. I'm shaking too badly to even attempt to walk, so I crawl.

In the wrong goddamn direction.

He watches me with every inch I gain, like a volcano ready to erupt. My cheek still stings with the memory of his slap, but I can't stop. The moment I'm close enough, his hand flies out, clenching my throat instead. Tight. He chokes me so hard that I see black. I'll bruise. Seconds pass. I'll die...

"Am I supposed to cry now, *kotyonok*?" he asks me mockingly, sounding miles away. "Tell you my sins? Beg for your forgiveness?"

Air floods my lungs as he shoves me aside like trash. I go limp, my cheek pressed against the ice-cold floor, his hate basting my skin. It feels different this time—everything. It's too real. Too sharp.

His voice inflicts more pain than any knife. Go figure.

"Please…" My throat aches in the wake of that word. What it means: pleading. I've begged before. I've begged Melanie not to go. I've begged men not to hurt me. I've begged landlords not to kick us out.

No one ever listens.

Maybe I never really meant it before now.

"What?" Maxim demands. "Please don't hurt you? Please don't kill you?" He laughs again and the vibration runs through the floor as he stands. Two steps bring him close enough for his foot to nudge my side. Hard. "Pleading didn't save my mother from her fate—"

"I'm not her—"

His foot rams into my side, knocking me onto my back.

Gasping, I can only stare up at him as he glares down. "You're not him."

"I'm not?" Slowly, his eyes track over the length of my body, narrowing as they reach the space between my legs. One of his hands reaches down to palm his cock, while the other…

From one of his pockets, he pulls out a knife and flicks his wrist, springing the blade free. Then he sinks to one knee, capturing my thigh in his other hand before I can attempt to scuttle away. In retaliation, his nails dig in, his breath searing my flesh, and he drags the blade between my legs.

There's no teasing this time. No taunts. He slides the blade along the outside of my pussy, nudging me open. A strangled gasp trickles between my lips as my hand flies out to bat his away.

"P-please."

He jerks his grip on the knife and the blade bites into my inner thigh, drawing a stream of blood that dribbles down, slicking his way.

"Spread your legs," he grates, his voice ragged. A hiss of anger leaves his mouth when I don't move quickly enough, and the blade cuts me again, another fiery line. "Do it."

The tarp clings to my skin as my legs drift apart to let his bulk fit in between them. He risks letting me go to grab his cock again, but even from this angle, I know he's still not hard. Not even when I flinch. Not even as tears sting behind my eyes and slide down my cheeks.

There's no way around it: Since meeting him, my pain alone isn't getting him off. His eyes are too haunted. I don't even think he's really here, but in the past. Trapped. Furious...

Terrified.

And I should say the goddamn safe word. My lips move, but nothing comes out, just whimpers. He lifts the knife and I raise my hand, pressing my palm against his cheek in one last bid for mercy. It takes everything I have to meet his gaze—to stare into his eyes and not cringe away at what I see.

"I don't want you to hurt me like this. I don't…I don't want to be afraid of you."

Confusion shatters the bitter expression, matching the emotion surging through me. It makes him look even more lost. Even more terrifying. More dangerous. He drags me beneath him, his weight crushing me against the hard floor.

"Do you think I won't?" he growls into my ear.

"*Don't.*" My knees rise up on either side of him while my other hand grabs his hip, breaking that unspoken rule. Bit by bit, some life returns to his eyes, but he doesn't pull away.

"Then do not let me go back there. To that place," he grits out. His eyes flutter, unseeing one second and alive the next. "Keep me here. I don't… I'm not him."

I don't know what he means until he lunges. His lips latch onto mine, kissing me. Biting me. He's ruthless, shoving his tongue into my mouth without giving me a chance to come up for air.

Benny only ever gave me one piece of advice when I started working for him: "*You want to get it over with? Let those fuckers think you want it. That you need it. It'll finish them off and you'll probably get a tip while you're at it.*"

I could never really pretend.

I've never been that desperate.

But this time…I don't have to think. Maybe I'm just too fucking chicken to die. I let myself cling to him, dragging my fingers through his hair, kissing him back—knowing that, at any second, he'll push me off. Kill me.

But all he does is come back to life. Restless and ragged, the fallen angel returns from hell with a vengeance. My body is his tool. His anchor. His altar.

Maybe it's way too easy to arch into him. Either way, I don't give myself the chance to think about it.

When he flips me onto my stomach, his kiss becomes something else. The lips pressed against the back of my shoulder don't reveal nipping teeth. They just graze my skin. They feel. They taste.

I don't know how much time passes before something else stabs between my legs, guided by his hand. I barely register the familiar shape before he's sliding inside me, fucking me deep with a groan: one part pleasure, one part relief.

Sweat and skin wrap me inside my own corner of the universe: a tiny sliver of hell. Warmth spills down my cheeks like fire as he finally thrusts in earnest.

Each slow buck of his hips desolates me. I was wrong. This isn't fucking—it's something else. Something more twisted than any torture he's inflicted upon me so far: *desperation.*

"You keep falling deeper," he murmurs into my throbbing skin, so softly that I probably imagined it. "Every fucking time I try to give you a way out. You refuse to take it."

Any reply escapes me as my stomach bunches into knots, my insides swirling into jelly.

"And I've tried to show you mercy." A hard, deep thrust sends my eyes rolling into the back of my head, making me cry. Making me scream around mouthfuls of plastic and blood. "I've tried… But if I can't eliminate you myself, I'll have no choice…"

With one last thrust, rivulets of heat spill into me.

All of him.

I'm swirling in a daze as his lips find my ear again, his voice rough. "I'll have no choice."

CHAPTER SEVEN

I wake up in my bed. No...*his* bed. When I finally peel my eyes open, there is no mistaking his domain. Ebony walls encase me, blending in with the black sheets and duvet that shield my body from the still air. One sharp inhale and I'm drowning beneath his scent.

Literally. Musk and sweat are a noose that asphyxiates me against layers of silk and satin. And blood.

I'm still bleeding from the cut on my back. Every part of me feels tender and sore. As cliché as the boast sounds, I won't be able to walk right for a few days.

Because he cut me.

My fingers slide beneath the blankets to feel the wounds for myself. The marks still smart, weeping and fresh. Only a few hours must have passed...

Which gives me plenty of time to come up with a new plan of action. When all else fails, there's always good old reliable plan B.

Run.

I roll onto my side first, biting a groan back as sores and wounds rip open. It's dark in the room. Maybe just after dawn, before the sun has fully risen. I know at a glance that Maxim isn't here, lurking within the corners. To be sure though, I crane my neck, straining my ears against the silence, and don't hear the sound of anyone in the rest of the suite, either.

Logic warns me to crawl into my bedroom and wait. Ride the contract out for as long as I can.

But, at the moment, my brain feels too fucking wrecked for logic.

Bit by goddamn bit, I wrestle my limbs into submission and crawl to the edge of the bed. When I finally manage to peel the covers back, I find that he left me naked. A quick scan of the room doesn't reveal my clothes anywhere. I have no choice but to limp over to his closet and wrench the sliding door to it open.

Any bravery I managed to muster up drains from me in one go. Even his clothing intimidates. Crisp dress shirts hang neatly in shades spanning black, navy, gray, and the purest white. My fingers shake as I grab one at random along with a pair of boxers. I pull both on while simultaneously staggering for the door.

He isn't in the foyer when I tiptoe across it. Neither do I hear him working in the sculpture room. His absence leaves an almost eerie, unnatural silence, broken only by my ragged breaths and the slight click of the front door when I finally pull it open.

I take the stairs down to the first floor and slip through a fire exit. Barefoot, I flag a cab down before realizing I don't have any money to pay the fare.

Go fucking figure.

Maybe the driver takes pity on me, because he sighs when I paw through the pockets of Maxim's shirt in a half-assed search for cash. "It's all right, miss." His eyes skim over my bruised, battered face and he quickly looks away before letting me off near a random street at the edge of Horn Hill. "Consider it on the house. Just take care of yourself out here."

This area is close to my old house. I should go back and regroup—think of a way to get the kids back home, if Maxim doesn't kick them out first. Or worse...

I start heading in that direction. But, somewhere along the way, I take a wrong turn and wind up in a back booth of some rundown diner. It's a slow time of day, right before the midmorning rush. A waitress patrols the aisles, brandishing a fresh pot of coffee. She offers to pour me a cup, but I shake my head and pray she'll walk away without looking at me twice.

Unlucky for me, I can't ignore my own fucking reflection. It's splashed over the metallic border of the window beside me. Splotches of blue and purple. Bits of garish red. I'm a fucking smorgasbord of color and wounds. I try smiling and look even worse.

It's only once I finally start to warm up beneath the building's artificial heat that I realize exactly what I'm doing: hiding out in the shitty part of town, wearing a madman's stolen dress shirt, and why? Because he hurt me. He scared me.

He's *scaring* me.

He's haunting me...

I look up when the bell above the door chimes and it's like his entrance is perfectly timed to create the most impact. At a glance, it's easy to tell that the figure entering the diner isn't the typical patron. His head is bowed, his face partially obscured by the hood of a gray sweatshirt, but his clothing is of the highest caliber, and his black boots are polished to a shine, clean enough to eat off of.

I'm already scrambling to the edge of my seat when his voice reaches me, a low but irresistible rasp.

"Don't run."

I've never heard him this coarse, absent of his usual poise. When I freeze, he jerks his head toward the table.

"Sit. We will talk. Can you give me that much, *kotyonok?*"

Can I?

My arms shake as I wrestle them around me, struggling to hide the shape of my body beneath his shirt. I picked white, of all fucking colors. Despite its quality, it's thin enough to see my nipples through. I've already stained it, too; streaks of red are blooming along my hip. Though maybe he won't miss it, considering how he switched up his style today.

I track every motion of his body as he claims the bench across from me and adjusts his bulk to fit within such a small space. His legs reach my side of the table, and he hunches over the width of the booth, his face so close that his breath scalds my cheek. That sweatshirt isn't the only change in his typical attire. Underneath it, he has on a gray tee-shirt that's soaked through with sweat. Drops of it glisten over his forehead as well and slick his hair back. Wherever he's been, he's been sweating. Sculpting? Working out?

His raw, bloodied knuckles give the answer away.

When he notices the line of my gaze, he casually tucks his hands into fists and moves them beneath the table. "So this is how you run, *kotyonok*?" He tilts his head just enough for me to see his face clearly through the shadow cast by the hood. "Frankly, I'm surprised. You seemed more like the type to press me for money before voiding your contract."

He's devastatingly polite, even in his harshest insults. *Press.* I know what he really means: *blackmail.*

But is he that far off base? Maybe not.

Any other time, I'd try to deny it. I'd pull out the main tricks Melanie always used in her arsenal. Bat my eyes.

Feign ignorance. I'd promise, never intending to keep a single goddamn word.

"You are afraid." The statement comes as the seconds tick by and I don't answer.

He's right. Fear is wired through my every nerve, and I nearly jump out of my skin when he reaches across the table. The pad of his thumb hesitates near the side of my face.

"I hit you," he says, eyeing the swollen welt beneath the black eye already there. "I apologize for that."

Shock could be blamed for the way I shudder, which makes him pull away in response. It's not every day that men —*anyone*—apologize to me.

The most terrifying part though? I think he means it.

Or maybe I'm just dumb enough—*desperate* enough—to believe him despite everything my life has taught me about the pervasive nature of violence. Apologies don't mop up blood. If my throbbing eye accounts for anything, they don't make your boo-boos magically feel better, either.

Though who the fuck knows? Again, I've never been presented with one before.

"I was rough," he adds, drawing my attention back to him. "But I don't think it will scar—"

"That's not the point." Of all the things clawing up my throat, desperate to be said, I don't expect what winds up spilling out. "I...I didn't sign up for this."

He sits up straighter as my voice breaks.

"And not the violence," I add as warmth spills down my face, impossible to stop. "You're a man. I've learned my whole life that men are violent pieces of shit—"

"We all ready to go?" Oblivious, the smiling waitress appears beside our table. She makes a show of convincing Maxim to order a cup of coffee, and—whether because he needs the caffeine or rather to just make her go away—he accepts two mugs, which the woman places between us.

As I watch the steam waft from the drink on my end of the table, I consider throwing it on him. Taking my chances. Running. But my own imagination isn't even on my side: I wouldn't make it very far.

His eyes narrow, honing in on the way I'm huddled against the back of my bench, as far from him as the space will allow. "Something tells me that this is about more than my..." He seems to mull over the nicest words to describe it: *more than my fucking loss of sanity.* "My brief lapse in composure."

Despite everything, I nearly choke out a scoff. *Composure*— that's what he calls it.

So what do you call it, Frankie? a part of me wonders. *What has you so fucking spooked? All you have to do is say the magic words...*

"I've shown you worse."

81

I stiffen at the accusation lurking within his tone. Almost a challenge: *I nearly beat you to death before and you stayed. Now, you run.*

"You threatened to kill me. You tried fucking someone else in front of me." My throat threatens to close up against those words. Gritting my teeth, I force more out. "I may like pain, but not like that."

"So," he says, his tone low and careful. "Are you saying you want to end this?"

He doesn't sound angry—that's the observation that worries me most of all.

"You don't throw away the people you say you want to keep." More tears. They come down like a fucking waterfall, blurring my vision. Within seconds, Maxim Koslov is a massive, indistinguishable shadow over red vinyl. "You told me... You said you'd never let me go." His words rasp over my tongue, nearly drowned out by the sudden laughter from a group of truckers seated two tables over. I let them linger in the air regardless, tasting their impact. Hearing them said out loud should mean something. It should resonate with some stubborn part of me that wants to bide my time.

He's a monster.

"I did," Maxim admits. Seconds pass without him saying anything else and I shift, attempting to stand.

"I-I don't know what you want."

"Wait—" His hand slams onto the table before I make it to the end of the booth. Gone is his blank mask of politeness. A feral fire flickers underneath, growing brighter with every word he grates to me next. "Let me explain. That night... You never looked like her," he rasps almost as if to himself. "Not until then. Like how she did. Her eyes..."

What are you talking about? That's what I try to say. A gasp crawls out of me instead. His face is in shadow, his body heaving, his breaths mingling with mine. My heart slows to a crawl; I've never been more terrified of him than I am right now.

He's never looked more human.

"I spent years telling myself that I wasn't like him," he says haltingly, as if picking the words one by one from some place deep inside himself. "It's the lie we feed ourselves as children, you see. The one we tell ourselves every fucking night. The same damn lie: *It could have been different.* If *they* were different. The world. You. Fuck, who knows? But you say it anyway, like a prayer: They could have changed. It could have been different..."

That dangerous, unstable edge creeps into his voice, triggering every flight response my body possesses. *Run, Frankie!* He's not talking about us in this moment. He's far away, beyond this room. Just when the panic becomes unbearable, he blinks and reality reels him back.

"Only now do I realize that it was just a fucking lie—" He forms a fist and smashes it against the table. His heavy sigh negates the violence of the act though. It's like he's too tired

83

to feel a damn thing. So he just bleeds, spilling more of himself in words than he ever could of my blood. "She would never leave him, even at his worst. She was broken. So was he. So am I. And so are you. You still hear that little voice yourself, don't you, *kotyonok*?" he wonders, flicking his gaze to my face. "'*Maybe I can change*,' it tells you. '*Maybe I won't be like her.*'"

I know just who he's referring to. *Melanie. Maybe I won't be like her...*

No. I want to shut him out. But he's speaking to a part of me too primal to control. The one place inside my soul that still thrives?

Unsatisfied with throwing me away, he has to kill the one thing of value I have left.

Hope.

"It's a lie, *kotyonok*," he says as if reading my mind. "You know it. So do I. It's inevitable. This is who we are. We're fucked, just like them. We will end, just like them. And do you know what else?" He laughs. "We will never change. Why? We do not want to. Hell, even now, you've yet to say your safe word."

"I want to say it now." The confession feels like the equivalent of striking a match over a pool of gasoline. One wrong move and the world will erupt in flames. Not for the first time, I have Maxim Koslov's full, rapt attention.

But, as the seconds race by, I'm starting to realize that the infantile plea wasn't directed at him. *Say it,* a part of me begs. Pleads. Desperation sets my throat on fire, burning no matter how much I swallow.

"I…I'm—"

"No, I owe you an explanation," Maxim says over me.

My eardrums pick up the subtle distinction, and curiosity steals my voice. *I owe you.* Not: *I want to give.*

"I forget that you are not used to this arrangement. You don't understand how it works." He makes it sound so complicated. So clinical. I'm a faulty piece in his cold, brutal machine of a life. "Your body is all I ever required from you," he clarifies. For a second, he gets that lost look again. Then he blinks, his gaze settling over my chest as if he can see my rapid heartbeat through paper-thin skin. "Nothing else."

His meaning takes an eternity to register. My body. *Sex.* Just sex. No moaning his name during said fucking, unbidden. No understanding his fucked-up childhood. No pitying him. Crying for him.

I wasn't supposed to glimpse the human beneath the monster's mask.

A funny sensation leaves me feeling dizzy—like he flipped the world upside down when I wasn't looking. Only he can do this to me: make me risk breaking my own damn rules. His past shouldn't matter. His fucked-up reasoning shouldn't matter. The pain that crosses his gaze for a brief moment *shouldn't* catch my attention.

Too late. My mouth opens. "So why keep me?"

He frowns, flexing his fingers as if flicking the question away. "I will make you an offer." In the blink of an eye, he's composed again. He scans the brightly colored upholstery behind my head as if the conversation is starting to lose his interest—but I'm not fucking fooled. One of his hands clenches the edge of the table, and the knuckles are stark white.

He waits, letting the gravity of the temptation sink in. Like the greedy bitch I am, I wait too, taking the bait. The devil is about to offer me another deal—and God, I should run.

"I'll let you go," he tells me, his eyes cutting into my own. "You can take the full amount in your contract, along with any extra owed to you. You will keep the house, and our arrangement will be null and void."

"Why?" I nearly choke on my confusion.

"I'm through with you," he says. "Don't think too much of it. It eventually happens with every woman I am involved with. Again, I will fulfill the payment promised in the contract."

It's a better offer than I could have ever asked for—in theory. But it doesn't feel that way. My chest aches like something tore through each rib, muscle, and bone. Maybe logic. Nothing in life comes without a pesky caveat: There's always a catch. I lick my lips, feeling them scrape against my tongue like broken glass. "If?"

He sits back against the booth, folding his hands before him. "Your pimp's name. What was it?"

Of all the people to be mentioned now. "Benny," I say.

"I remember now. Benjamin Ireland." He nods and steeples his fingers. "You will tell him that you will never work for him again. In exchange, you may stay in the home I've bought for you. However, I expect you to maintain our confidentiality."

I know what he really means: I stay away from any other man and keep his dirty, bloody secrets.

"And if I don't?" My breath catches, and my imagination takes off again. I picture him taking a new toy, fucking her on my bed—no. *His* bed.

Would he call her *kotyonok*?

"Tell me something." He leans forward, his accent thick, his breaths drifting across the table, heavy and hot. "And you do not want to lie to me now." He reaches out, cupping my chin, holding me captive, and I can sense the danger coiled in his touch, barely restrained. "What you said. That I'm not like… You were pretending, hmmm?"

I flinch as his thumb grazes a path over my throbbing cheek, deceptively soft, as if to coax the truth out.

"To save your life. I can forgive you that much," he says, "*if* you admit it."

My heart lurches in my chest. Of course I was lying. I *was…*

"I see." His hand withdraws, curling into a fist that he quickly shoves into his pocket. "I will give you a week to make your decision." He stands, leaving his untouched cup of coffee there on the table. "You can have the money in the meantime. My protection. The house. All of it. Return to your normal life if you want. Live as you would away from me."

I'm holding my breath—even before he tacks on the dreaded *but*.

"*But* I ask that you obey my request." His eyes find mine, drilling in the unspoken threat.

This isn't a negotiation. I know there's no point in arguing. Still, I lick my lips and choke out, "Can I ask why?"

"You are naïve," he says as though it's the most obvious explanation. "My enemies wouldn't be above fucking you for leverage."

In other words: *You're a liability.*

"And what about you?" My teeth chatter as if they're fighting to keep this line of questioning locked away. It's a dangerous, stupid game to play. But fuck it, he's the one who called me a masochist. "Will you get someone else?"

To fuck.

To toy with.

To beat?

He looks away while rummaging through the pockets of his sweatshirt. After a few seconds, he tosses a bill onto the table. "Stay. I'll arrange to have you taken home. Consider the house yours to do with as you wish. Lucius will settle your finances." He lingers near the booth, casting a silence that seems to ensnare the entire fucking café in a net of tension. There is more he wants to say. Confirmation of my suspicion?

No matter what he wants me to do, he *will* get a new woman.

He *will* fuck someone else.

And there isn't a damn thing I can do about it.

Why?

He is the dominant master, drawing eyes from every single patron as he heads for the door.

I'm the invisible, worthless submissive: a cheap whore, easily thrown away. He may have let me keep my dollhouse, but that's all I'm worth to him.

A bribe.

Hours must pass after he leaves, but I just sit here, staring at the empty seat across from me. When I finally slink out of the diner, it's dark out.

But there, idling just alongside the curb, is a familiar black car. The driver meets my gaze through the windshield and nods just once in a silent gesture. *At your service.*

CHAPTER EIGHT

I've been thrown away so many times.

This latest trip to the figurative dumpster should be nothing new. My own mother didn't want me. What difference should the whims of a psycho billionaire make?

Not a one.

Despite knowing that, I can't escape the pins-and-needles sensation stabbing at my spine, warning me that something isn't right. This time *is* different. Psycho billionaires just don't throw away their wayward pets who scratch too deep and leave a mark—no, they put them to sleep.

And every passing second feels like the tightening coil of a trap. I know it will spring without warning. Maxim will step out from the shadows and demand some cruel punishment for ever leaving him.

I'll lose this twisted game.

In the meantime, I spend each night sleeping in an unfamiliar bed before wandering around an unfamiliar house to get the kids ready for school. A new *private* school they were mysteriously enrolled into, despite it being the middle of the fucking school year. I expect them to resent me for the change. To hate me for ripping them from the house—*our* house—without any real explanation.

Ainsley should be pouting.

Mikie and Daisy should be bitching about missing their old friends or their old neighborhood.

Ollie, Ray, and Eric should be pining for their old beds, their old rooms.

Instead, it's like we've lived here all along. Like we weren't fighting over scraps of pizza just a few weeks ago. Like they *always* could relax on their front lawn without worrying about some gangbanger cutting loose.

Survival is a funny thing.

"Frankie?"

I jump as a hand lands over my shoulder and the plate I'm holding falls back into the water-filled sink. It smacks the edge wrong and promptly breaks into a million expensive chunks of porcelain.

"Shit!" I shut the water off and try to fish the broken pieces from the sink, being careful to avoid cutting myself. The jagged edges are sharp. The slightest nudge with my fingertip causes a faint echo of pain. A hint of it—but a firmer nudge sends a tendril of agony shooting down my spine.

"Are you okay?" Daisy presses when I don't acknowledge her right away. Little does she know, she just asked the question of the fucking day. "Frankie?"

"Yeah…sure," I hear myself croak as my fingers plunge into the soapy water and clumsily grab at another chunk. It cuts me deeper this time and a brief flash of red fades through the water. "Why?"

"You've been washing the same three knives and plates for the past hour. And," she adds, her voice quivering as she watches me wrench my bleeding hand from the water and shove it into the nearest dish towel, "That's the fifth plate you've broken since you got here."

"Oh." I let the word hang there, a perfect summary of the past few days.

Oh, my fingers slipped.

Oh, I'm bleeding.

Oh, it doesn't hurt.

"I'm okay," I force myself to choke out when Daisy doesn't move, her unsaid questions itching my skin. "It…it doesn't even hurt."

"Okay." In her small voice, a heavy sigh somehow sounds louder than even the few times she manages to shout. "Well… I have to finish my homework…" Her eyes drift hopefully in my direction. "Are you busy?"

Busy. My brain toys with that word. Busy? For once, I'm not. I'm not scraping by at some shitty job for low wages. Or on my knees pleasing a horny stranger for cash. It's been so long since I've been able to stay in the same house with the kids and not race to get ready for the next dead-end job.

"No." I step away from the sink and wipe my hands on my shirt. "Sure… I can help."

"Cool!" Daisy beams and I catch myself staring. It's the first time I've really seen her smile in so damn long. "It's just math," she says, leading me to a section of the dining room, cordoned off by a pink backpack and a mound of books. "Algebra." She rolls her eyes and gestures to an open workbook. "Think you can help? I hate equations."

I scan the scrambled mixture of numbers and letters printed on the sheet and squint. Algebra? It's like another fucking language.

"What about this one?" Daisy points to a cluster of symbols. "I need to solve for X but I have no idea where to start."

"X?" I raise an eyebrow. "Isn't math supposed to be about numbers?"

"Never mind." Daisy closes her workbook and starts to shove it into her backpack. "I'll ask Mikie—"

"No! I can help." I practically snatch the notebook from her hands and flip to a random page. None of it makes sense. "I… Do you have a calculator—"

"I said it's fine." Daisy grabs her book but rather than put it away, she clutches it to her chest, eyeing me warily. "Can I ask you something?"

"Sure," I croak. But I look away and eye the table rather than her. "You can ask me anything."

"Okay... Well, you've been acting really weird lately, you know?"

"Weird?" I choke back a laugh. *Weird,* or just too fucking stupid to solve a math problem. "How?"

"Weird like bringing a scary guy home," Daisy says. "Weird like moving us into a mansion overnight. Weird like—"

"Hey!"

I look over my shoulder and see Mikie there, a game controller in hand.

"You coming back?" he asks Daisy. "I'm about to crush this level."

"Not yet." She sighs again. "We were trying to do homework." She's still smiling, but it's lopsided. Strained.

"I can help," Mikie says, strolling over. "Let's see it. Oh yeah, this shit is easy. X is twelve." He pumps his fist in triumph. "Need help with more? Come on. I'll help ya. I bet Frankie's too tired for algebra anyway."

"Thanks for trying," Daisy says, following in Mikie's wake. "Night, Frankie."

"Night," I echo, but when I finally turn around, I realize I'm alone. Which is a funny emotion to feel in a house with six other people.

Our new house isn't the only change the kids have seemed to easily overlook.

Apart from Daisy, it's like they don't even see the battered, bruised excuse they have for a sister, either. I'm dripping blood, spouting off excuses like Band-Aids. The lies I tell to explain the injuries away are easily accepted, too—but with a catch. They avert their eyes and nod a little more than necessary, which is the same way I used to accept Melanie's lies. The ones I was too damn tired to challenge. Even Mikie doesn't question me. As far as they're concerned, I'm still the same old Frankie. The same old nagging, sole-providing, fight-breaking, rule-setting fucking Frankie.

Barely five minutes go by without me having to separate Ainsley and Eric, clean something, fix something, or wipe something from the floor. I bust my ass to erase every speck of dust and dirt they leave behind.

Because we don't really belong here.

I don't belong here.

But at least money is the furthest thing from my mind now, right?

I try to tell myself that over and over, hoping that it might stick this time. Maxim may be a lot of things, but I don't think a *liar* is one of them, at least where finances are concerned. And if I am anything like my mother, I'll milk him for all he's worth for as long as I fucking can.

In the end, I last three days. Three damn days before the walls of the house start closing in. Three days before my own skin starts to shrivel around me. Three days that I can't even fucking look at myself in the mirror.

I'm a sleepwalker in a dream, observing myself in the bathroom for cracks in my porcelain skin.

Then I hear it—a sound that shatters my daze: crying. Screaming.

"Frankie!"

Horror sends my stomach plummeting as I race downstairs into the entryway. "What's wrong?"

I find Daisy huddled on the bottom step. Spotting me, she lurches to her feet, tears streaming down her pale cheeks.

"What's wrong?" I demand, grabbing her by the shoulders.

Her eyes dart to the front entrance and reality returns like a bitch-slap. We're not alone.

Two men dressed in blue police uniforms guard the open door while another man in an impeccable suit stands in the middle of the room, radiating authority. Lucius.

My heart stops. *Me.* They're here for me. Maxim may be a self-professed crime lord, but I'm not.

And I committed murder.

"Ms. Marconi." Lucius steps forward, his dark eyes laced with concern. "I apologize for this sudden—"

"She's dead," Daisy blubbers over him. "Mama... She's dead."

I blink. My first thought is who? It's almost like one of those game show songs is playing as my brain slowly connects the dots. *Mama. Mom. Mother.*

Oh. Finally, my tongue wrings out a name. "Melanie?"

"Yes. They found her this morning!" Daisy wails against my shoulder. I have enough sense to throw my arms around her neck, holding her close. She's still wearing her pajamas, her hair in two braids. "I-I don't know how—"

"It's best if we discuss this in private," Lucius interjects. "In fact, I would have preferred to deliver this news myself." He cuts his gaze to the officers.

"It's an open investigation," one of them curtly replies.

Like it's that hard to guess the cause of death. I've had at least ten previous overdose scares to serve as a dress rehearsal for this moment. Some concerned passerby found her dead on a bench or in an alley, I bet. She slipped away high off her ass, without a concern to bother her pretty little head. My only consolation is that the kids didn't find her.

"Go to your room." I slide my arms from around Daisy and nudge her toward the stairs. "Go. I'll be up in a bit. Everything's fine."

Even I can hear the lie in my voice. Still, she heads for the stairs, and Lucius moves to stand beside me, taking her place.

"I suggest you say nothing, Ms. Marconi," he says.

"Is that really necessary?" One of the officers sighs. "We would just like to ask a few questions—"

"I suggest you direct all inquiries to Ms. Marconi's legal counsel," Lucius interjects. "I can facilitate a meeting, but as for now, gentlemen, I'm sure this family would like privacy."

"I don't think we can leave just yet." The other officer steps forward, twisting a pen between his fingers, a notepad in hand. He's young, with dark hair and piercing eyes. "Can you tell us the last time you saw Melanie Ryder alive, Francesca?" he asks. "We have a witness that claims the two of you had an argument recently. Can you elaborate?"

My mind goes blank, and I don't know how to describe the emotion that washes over me. It starts in my stomach, pinching like hell as I try to identify it. "I—"

"I suggest you save the questions for another day," a newer voice cuts over mine.

Both officers share wary glances before eyeing the newest figure to enter through the doorway. Dressed in black and shrouded in an ebony coat, Maxim Koslov exudes an aura of intimidation not even they can ignore.

"Sorry to interrupt." His gaze passes over me, finding Lucius. They share a silent nod, and Maxim crosses his arms. "But if you wouldn't mind, gentlemen, I believe Ms. Marconi should process this devastating news alone."

"This is an open investigation," the man with the notepad counters. "I can't just ignore protocol..."

Maxim doesn't say a single word, but the officer grits his teeth and then shoves his pen into his pocket. "Fine."

The other officer concedes with a curt nod. "Goodnight."

As they leave, Lucius follows. "I'll handle this," he says to Maxim.

The door closes behind them and I'm trapped. Within seconds, his scent easily overpowers that of six kids and a nanny. Three days without him have strengthened it. My pathetic brain hones in on the chilling familiarity of it over all else. Primal, raw musk. As long as I breathe it in, there isn't room for anything more.

"For now, I think you should avoid the police," he says, his voice low—out of respect for the kids, I realize. "I wanted Lucius to tell you before they could."

Belatedly, his words register—and what they reveal.

He wanted Lucius to tell me. Not *him*.

I cross to the other end of the foyer and eye the view beyond the window. It's late, way past sunset. Storm clouds darken the ebony sky, and lightning flashes between them. Of all the days to die, Melanie sure picked a winner.

Though, there goes my park bench theory; Melanie hated the rain.

A motel then, I surmise. They found her sprawled out in one with a needle in her vein. I've entertained that scenario as well, though not as often as the others—because a motel overdose means publicity. Her name might show up in the paper. Publicity means investigations, long and drawn out.

Investigations during which a dumb, worthless whore might say the wrong thing, casting suspicion on her billionaire client who relishes his privacy.

That's why he's here.

"I'm not going to say anything about that guy I…"

Killed. The word sticks in my throat. I still can't say it out loud.

"I won't go to the police," I confess to the window. "That would bring my sister into it. I'd never do that to her."

Even if I were spiteful enough to mention his name.

There. He should be satisfied…

But his footsteps don't echo to signal a retreat.

"Do you need me to sign something?" I ask, wringing my fingers together. They're shaking, and each nail nips at any bit of skin it can reach. A pinch here. A scratch there. I watch the blood bubble up from miniscule scrapes, but it's strange. I feel nothing.

"No," he says finally. "Lucius will handle your legal counsel."

"Okay." I sound like the perfect obedient hostage, meekly abiding by his rules. "Thank you."

I turn to face him, ready to keep up my act. Go upstairs. Lock myself in my cage. Let him see how well I can play the role of damaged, unwanted toy.

But his face is all wrong. His gaze is solely focused on me, his posture rigid, his eyes unnervingly sharp. A million secrets lurk in them, daring me to question.

"How...how did she die?" I croak before I can bite the words back.

"She was stabbed. They found her in a home in Horn Hill. The coroner will rule it a homicide. There are no leads..." He trails off, a blond eyebrow raised. "Hearing this upsets you."

No. I shake my head, unable to push a denial past my thickening throat. Upset? I'm not. Those aren't tears searing my eyes. Just dust. He must have been sculpting before he came here. The air is fucking thick with heavy, cloying residue.

"What else?" I ask.

"They will not release her body for a few days, at least until the investigation is concluded. However...I believe it would be best to schedule a memorial service anyway. Closure for your siblings. If you'd like, I can make the arrangements."

Closure. Siblings. My siblings.

The strangest thought makes me laugh brokenly. "You knew. Of course you knew!" Exhaustion robs my voice of its dramatic flair. I just sound fucking tired. "For how long?"

"Since yesterday morning." He doesn't even deny it. "She was initially a Jane Doe, but I had my suspicions. They identified her officially late last night."

"But you didn't tell me then. You were going to have Lucius tell me instead." And not out of oversight. I've become well-versed in the nuances of Maxim Koslov lately. He does nothing without calculated interest. "Like I said, I won't go running to the police. So you can stop pretending like you even give a shit—"

"You're upset." A warning laces his tone, soft like a trip wire waiting to be sprung.

"No." I exhale, running my fingers through my hair. "I'm... *You* ended our contract. That means you don't get to control—"

"I wanted to give you more time." He grabs my wrist and I flinch as every nerve goes haywire beneath my skin. *Zap!*

It's funny. Melanie always went back to heroin no matter how many fucking times she overdosed, and I hated her for it. But now, with his touch on my skin, I think I know why. Oblivion is so much better than cold, cruel reality—and it takes everything I have in me to pull away.

Even more shocking? He lets me.

"Time to what?"

The answer lurks in the tentative way he held me. Not hard and punishingly like I'm used to. Softer. Gentler. Comforting?

"Time to think."

I shake my head. "I don't want to think!"

I need to act. Do something. Hug the kids, maybe? Call around for funeral homes. Normal people send out announcements when a family member dies, I think. Go figure, I can't think of a single person to announce Melanie's demise to. Maybe the deadbeat boyfriends eager to pay their last respects? Or all the bill collectors that will undoubtedly come calling? Or I bet she has a mound of debt waiting to be shackled to her next living descendant.

"Breathe—"

"I'm not upset." My voice falls flat, echoing in the cavernous room around us.

Shadows stretch across the floor, swallowing us in their path. Thunder echoes beyond the walls, faint but distant. Like memories, in a way. Those old, blurry ones from my childhood, back when I might have felt something other than hate for Melanie. Something instinctual and pathetic that I assume every child has either nurtured or squashed by those around them. Love?

My love for her, if it ever existed, is now long gone. Dust.

Like the particles swirling in the air, making my eyes water and my throat constrict. This fucking dust.

"I'm fine—"

"Fine," he says without argument.

My heart pounds harder. Thoughts race. Too many things battle for attention. Melanie. Death. Melanie. Funerals. Arrangements. The kids. Maxim. Maxim. Maxim…

"I'll handle the arrangements," he says, flicking the collar of his coat. "Goodnight."

He heads for the door before I can say anything else.

When he leaves, he doesn't look back.

Not once.

DING, dong, the witch is dead. I should designate the date a personal holiday. But Mommy dearest always had to have the last laugh: I'm the one still paying for her mistakes.

Lately, it feels like there are two Francescas, both superficial copies. One is a lapdog who used to pine at her master's feet. The other is a pseudo *mother-chef-referee-office worker-consultant-grief counselor-banker-always-has-everything-together, no-shit-taker.*

I'm not sure which woman is easier to be. I'm not even sure which one I like being more. Maybe it's the mask that requires no real effort on my part to wear?

The pet who just lies there as she's walked over, used, and screwed.

Or maybe it's the performance that makes me feel—even for a little while—like someone worth being.

As long as I continue to *do*, and *be*, and *have* everything.

At least in one of those roles, I don't have to smile as much. Here, trapped inside the house Maxim bought for my family, my lips are always contorted on cue. Voila. I'm caring, loving sister Frankie, ready to comfort, and hug, and offer reassurance that everything will be okay, as long as I'm here.

We don't need *her* and never have.

I approach the living room, determined to put on a convincing act. I can hear faint sobbing even from here— Daisy probably. Sure enough, I round the corner and find her slumped on a leather couch, with Mikie by her side. At her feet, Ainsley is body-slamming Eric to the floor, while the twins, Ollie and Ray, trade insults over a video game playing on the television.

"Bet you can't beat my score—"

"Bet your ass I can!"

"Fuck off!"

As the bickering continues, I sense my nails dig into the inside of my wrist, pinching. Gouging. I look down, recognizing the bright-red substance seeping from the tiny scratches, but the burning sting I should feel is nothing more than a dull ache.

Am I dreaming? Inside a parallel universe? One where up is down and down is up and dead mothers still exist?

"Hey, Frankie," Mikie calls, drawing my attention. A frown tugs at his mouth, but otherwise, he looks fine.

In fact…everything feels so fucking normal.

Except Daisy. Her sniffling could signal yet another of her daily dramas—if it weren't for what she has clutched to her chest.

My eyes hone in on it, narrowing. It's a photograph, framed in one of those popsicle-stick frames you make in kindergarten. A photo only she would keep, long after I'd tossed out every other picture of this person in particular. The strange woman smiles up at me from between Daisy's splayed fingers. With dark, curling hair and brown eyes, she looks like me—long before she took to dying her hair and caking makeup over her face. She looks so damn young. I can't stop staring.

I can't stop seeing that handmade frame as a goddamn mirror, reflecting everything I am now back at me.

Tired. Desperate. Pathetic.

"Oh, look!" Eric exclaims, ramming his elbow into Ainsley's stomach. "Suck it—"

"Mikie!" Ainsley whines while the twins burst into a shouting match over their game.

All I can think to say is, "I… Can everyone shut up?"

Silence descends as suddenly as if I flipped a switch. I can think, finally. I can hear. Daisy's sniffling. Ainsley muttering. Mikie standing.

"Frankie?"

"You…you do know that she's dead?"

They all stare up at me, six blank faces, only one streaked with tears.

"*Melanie*," I correct harshly. "You know Melanie is dead, don't you?"

"Yeah." Mikie nods and glances at the younger kids. "It's sad, but I don't want us to focus on it—"

"She was stabbed to death," I spit out. Oops. It's the wrong thing to say.

"Frankie!" Mikie slaps his hands over Ainsley's ears.

She immediately attempts to shrug him off. "Let go!" she shrieks, only to have Mikie slap his hand over her mouth, too.

"Are you really doing this right now?" he asks.

"Why would you say that, Frankie?" Daisy lurches from the couch, still clutching that damn picture to her chest. "Why the hell would you say that?"

"It's the truth." God, I don't even recognize the sound of my voice. I'm not used to sounding this cold. This callous. Like…

Like Maxim.

"She's dead—"

"Shut up!" Daisy's voice rises to a whistle-like pitch, her cheeks splotched and red. "Why are you here? Why is she even here?" she demands, turning to Mikie. "It's not like you really give a shit anyway, right, Frankie? You're never fucking here!"

"What are you talking about?" Genuine confusion has me frowning. "I'm always here."

Always. Even when most people my age would have bailed on the responsibility. Long after Melanie *did* bail. I've always been here.

"Are you?" Daisy steps in closer, her arms wrapped tightly around the picture frame.

Up this close, I'm struck by just how different we look—not like siblings at all. She's blond-haired. There are no cuts on her wrists or scratches on her fingers. She doesn't share the empty, dull expression of the woman in the photograph.

I can't stop myself from reaching for it. My fingers only manage to snag the end of a popsicle stick before the whole damn thing snaps.

"Stop it!" Daisy rears back. "What did you do?"

"Everyone calm the hell down!" Mikie positions himself between me and Daisy, his palms outstretched to opposite ends. "Everyone just relax—"

"No!" Daisy pushes past him, her arms wrapped around that goddamn picture. "I don't want her here. It's not like she really cares anyway," she blubbers. "Do you? Or maybe you're glad, huh? Maybe now you can stop trying to be her—"

I don't register the slap until the moment my palm connects with the smooth skin of Daisy's cheek. The resounding thwack echoes like a gunshot. Suddenly, it's too damn quiet.

"Frankie, what the hell?" Mikie rushes toward Daisy, dragging her back.

She stares at me, her mouth open in shock. Even now, she's still holding that goddamn picture.

You don't care, do you?

But does anyone, really? I glance around the room and surmise the answer on my own. No. No one really gives a shit. Our mother is dead, but it might as well be another day. Another fucking Sunday. Another goddamn, grueling, unbearable day.

Do I care?

I should. The shackles that have weighed me down for so damn long should have fallen off the moment she drew her last breath. Daisy's right: I don't have to be her anymore. I don't have to fill her shoes. I don't have to wear her mask and be all those things she never was.

The bitch is dead; I *should* be free.

"Frankie?"

The soothing color scheme of the living room blurs into gray as I whirl on my heel and ignore the hand that paws at my shoulder.

"Where the hell are you going?"

I open my mouth to answer, but nothing comes out. Somewhere.

Anywhere.

I just need air. Ironically, I don't find any when I finally wrench the front door open. My lungs expand on nothing. I can't catch my breath, no matter how quickly I race down the walkway. Up ahead, a car waits and the driver stands at the back seat door, ready to usher me inside.

"Ms. Marconi?" He clears his throat pointedly when I start past him, reminding me of my unspoken boundary. Even thrown away and exiled, I'm still on a leash. "Ms. Marconi?"

I walk faster, inching toward the gate that bars this wealthy community from the outside world. Then I keep going, following a path that cuts through a scenic park, toward god knows where.

I'm not running.

Maybe I'm still looking for that elusive fresh air? Everything I breathe in feels tainted. Dirty. Dusty.

A bit like my soul.

Melanie was always a stain inside me, seeping through flesh and bone. Like a fool, I always believed that her inevitable death might act like soap and scrub it clean. Everything I've done—the worst, most disgusting acts—has been because of her.

Or has it?

Desperate to regain my bearings, I collapse on a random bench, cradling my aching head in my hands.

She's gone.

I have to say it out loud, just to hear the way it sounds. Hollow—that's how. Melanie is dead, but I...

I'm not.

"Here."

I flinch as a white strip of fabric appears in front of my face, offered from above by someone behind me. A shadow fans out before I can react, painting the pavement black as I sense a presence settle onto the narrow bench. I look over and find Maxim seated there, staring resolutely ahead. It stopped raining hours ago, but the stench of it still taints the air. Odd. I can finally inhale it now, tasting the nuances of the past storm and the evening chill.

"I just needed some air—"

"You do not have to lie to me."

My lips seal together, a slave to his command. Don't lie. I might as well say nothing ever again. It's all I fucking seem capable of lately.

I'm fine.

I'm fine.

I'm fine.

"Are you going to be watching me forever?" I wonder. "Waiting to jump the second you think I won't play by your rules?"

I don't receive an answer. Just as well, I'm used to responding to myself these days.

"I'm so tired of everyone treating me like a punching bag, or a piggy bank, or a toy." Oops. The confession spills out of me, hot and raw. I grit my teeth, biting back more— but it's like a dam breaking. Boom. Everything spills loose. I'm on my feet before I realize, pacing on the path of grass beside the pavement. "How could she do this to me? How could she be so fucking selfish?" A strangled sound cuts off the tirade. God no. My eyes are on fire. I reach up to rub them, but shit, the motion just triggers an avalanche. I'm sobbing in no time, gasping. "I hate... I hate her!"

Someone grabs me harshly, spinning me into a wall of muscle. Maxim. His smell trickles down my nostrils, tripping every nerve on the way down. The nearness stings, like touching a hot stove, and I instinctively jerk out of his reach.

"Get off of me!"

He doesn't move, but a slight tensing of his jaw conveys a silent warning. I'm making a scene. Even now, there are people out strolling the paths, enjoying this quiet hour just before dusk. They giggle and gossip, oblivious to the crime lord casting a shadow over this secluded corner.

He's a demon painted red in the glow of the blood-red sky. The sinking sun ignites the horizon, adding a chilling backdrop to his gaze. It's beautiful. And terrifying. Taken altogether, he's a striking contrast: smooth ebony silk and impenetrable flesh.

"You're in shock," he murmurs in a tone that makes my blood run cold. Maybe he's talking that way because he's never seen me like this: crying, sobbing. He's never seen the disgusting shell of Francesca Marconi his pretty dresses and bruises used to disguise.

"I'm fine."

"Look at me." His nails capture the underside of my jaw as his body moves in, nearly knocking me over to keep me close this time. Trapped.

My lips part, ready to deliver my customary response. *I'm fine.* It's right there on the tip of my tongue.

"I-I'm so tired." *Fuck.* My cheeks burn, but nothing can snatch the answer back. It's there, lingering on the air. "I'm so fucking tired. I'm so tired."

Of what?

He doesn't need to ask the question out loud—his grip tightens, wringing the confession from me.

"I'm so tired of pretending and being everything for everyone. I'm so..." Another sob triggers a burning rush of tears. They sink into the front of his shirt, alerting me to just how close he is—no longer entirely of his doing, either. My hands snuck against his abdomen without my realizing, seizing handfuls of his coat. I flinch, forcing my fingers to open, letting him go.

"I just... I don't want to be like her!" I'm channeling Daisy in her most dramatic of fits now, choking back sobs and sniffling snot. "I don't want to be like her anymore."

Lost.

Useless.

Worthless.

"I'm so tired of taking care of everyone all the time. I just want—"

"What?" He grabs my chin again, forcing it back so that I have no choice but to face him.

"I want...to be free," I hear myself croak. Though what the fuck does that mean? "I want..." My brain overloads and stalls like a crashing computer. Rebooting takes a few breathless seconds as I watch him watch me. "I just want something that's mine. Something that I can have for myself. I don't have to pretend. I'm not her. She never did anything useful. All she did was screw people over and..."

Survive. Just like me.

There are so many things she wasn't. Successful. A good mother. Happy. "She never went to school. I couldn't, either. She never made something of herself without fucking someone else over. But what have I done? Bedtime stories, money for field trips, the rent! She never took care of any of these things and still Daisy thinks she walks on water. I sacrificed everything! And for what? To be someone's whore? A pet? It's not like I'm made for anything better. God! I couldn't even help Daisy with Algebra—"

"Education," Maxim says over me. "Is that what you want?"

I blink. Like any delinquent, I have my GED, but beyond that?

Before I can answer, he sighs. "Consider it done. As payment for your continued silence. Stay here." He steps away, adjusting his coat. "I will have Lucius come for you."

He turns and advances down the path without an invitation for me to follow.

And I've never felt more alone.

CHAPTER NINE

Melanie never spoke about what she wanted when she died, at least not around me. Funny, because we damned each other to hell on a daily basis, but I don't even know if her body belonged in a church.

We could be Jewish for fuck's sake.

Regardless, Maxim takes over the "arrangements," leaving me blissfully in the dark. Good. Would knowing she's in the ground, tainting the earth, be any better than having her ashes on the mantel while the kids played on the floor beneath?

It's one of the myriad of things I don't want to think about —but Maxim's taken careful steps to reinforce his previous promise: he handles it all.

I can hear the kids being marshaled, presumably by Lucius, and ushered out the front door of the house. So I stay, trapped within a room like one from a fairytale. A deranged, twisted story in which the innocent victim isn't really all that innocent. Her monster prepared a special place for her in his substitute lair: one with white walls and carpeting and a bed with a gossamer canopy. But in the end, it's nothing more than a cage. A way to keep her separated from his real dwelling.

She's expendable.

"Ms. Marconi?"

"Coming." My heart pounds furiously as I follow the direction of the voice and find Lucius in the living room.

"The au pair took the children out for dinner," he explains. "I hope you don't mind. Also, Mr. Koslov asked me to bring you this."

He extends an object in my direction, and I warily accept it. It's flat, like a book. A brochure? On the front is an ivy-covered building underneath text proclaiming a name I vaguely recognize. One of the city colleges?

I look up, eyeing him warily. "He's serious?"

He can't be.

Lucius nods. "Should you accept, he will handle the tuition. Pick your courses. Tomorrow, you go for the preliminary tests."

"He can't be serious." I sound like a broken record—emphasis on the broken. Something seeped into my voice without permission. Terror?

Men like Maxim do nothing without expecting more in return.

Looking at Lucius' stoic expression, I can't tell what the price is this time.

"He doesn't have to bribe me to stay silent," I say in a rush.

Lucius raises an eyebrow. "I'm not sure what you mean, miss."

"I...I don't even know what to study." I never had the time to wonder before. In fact, the only "educational pursuit" I'd probably be good at is business management, all things considered.

"Have you changed your mind?"

I stiffen, shaking my head. "N-no. I just—"

"Then I will come for you tomorrow." He nods curtly and heads for the door. "Oh, and my condolences for your loss. Your mother's memorial service is tonight." An uncharacteristic emotion colors his voice. Hesitation? "All you have to do is arrive."

Arrive, most likely, to a funeral home, where some priest will give her the pomp and circumstance she never gave me, let alone any of the kids.

"Don't you think this is moving too fast?" I hate how fucking breathless I sound. Weak. "I mean, d-do the police even know who killed her—"

"Mr. Koslov thought it would be best to move quickly to give your siblings closure," he explains. "Her body hasn't been released, but a drawn-out investigation can be...taxing on some. He thought this way would be easier. Unless..." He furrows his eyebrows. "Do you not want to go?"

My teeth descend into my lower lip as I rebel against the obvious answer. Good daughters would attend their mothers' funerals, even if they hated them. Even if they wished them dead on a daily basis. Even if...

That "good" daughter sees her mother's smug fucking face wherever she looks, haunting her. Taunting her. *Don't you see, baby?* she croons from the grave. *We're the same...*

"I can convey your wishes to Mr. Koslov if that is so."

"No." My cheeks burn in the aftermath of the confession. It's like I've said a dirty word. "I don't think I need to. I mean..."

"All right." Lucius nods. "That just gives you more time to study." The reminder is paired with a deliberate nod toward the brochure still clutched in my fist. "Have a good evening, Miss Marconi."

After he leaves, I curl up on a leather chaise, tucking my legs beneath me. At first glance, the brochure looks like a typical overview of the average college campus. Numb, I flip through the first few pages, only to realize that the latter half is a summary of information for an entrance exam. English. Math. Spelling. All those subjects that feel like distant relics from high school.

Because I did so fucking good back then. My eyes squint as I run over the various subjects. Some jackass had the nerve to insert "general knowledge" in there somewhere, as if geography and the shape of fucking clouds are something everyone knows. The only thing that makes somewhat sense is math. Maybe because it's all I ever excelled at—a bitch who couldn't count her money right had no business hooking, after all.

I try my hand at the practice questions at the very back of the booklet. Wrong. Wrong. Wrong. It's like playing a game of how badly I can fuck up, proving something I've always known. Hell, even Melanie told me once that I'd only ever excel at one thing: lying on my back.

And plain fucking lying.

CHAPTER TEN

I would sell my soul in a heartbeat to keep my family safe. I used to tell myself that. I used to say it out loud. Once, I even shouted it at Melanie when she'd had the nerve to bitch about the sacrifices she made, having her children so young. "High school," she'd scoffed. "You had it easy. I didn't get to do any of that shit."

Fuck her. That bitch never knew the meaning of sacrifice. But do I? It's turning out to require more than I ever thought it would. Surrender is beyond enduring someone else's abuse, apparently.

It's having them ask you to *like* it.

It's believing that you might even *need* it…

It's letting yourself fall without even trying to safely land.

Only now am I starting to understand that I never really had to sacrifice anything, either. Nothing that really matters, anyway. Despite all the hell I've been through, I've always still been Frankie. Jaded, bitter, desperate, defiant, fucked-up, fucking Francesca Marconi.

No one had ever asked me to stop *being* her before. They never had anything to offer in exchange: namely all the shit I always told myself I never needed. Security. Safety...

I've given up so fucking much for my family over the years, but I'm not sure if I can leave that girl behind. Go figure. She's been the only bitch I could rely on.

Hell, Maxim easily found another toy.

And yet I remain in his dollhouse.

The obvious expense of the place seems eerie now. Alone in the living room, my breaths echo: shallow rasps echoing off the walls. I see myself. No matter where I look, my reflection gazes up at me from the polished floors. Only it's not *mine* entirely, but a woman who looks like me. Her eyes are wide and mocking, her hair a tangled mess.

Don't worry, baby, she tells me, snickering. It doesn't seem to faze her that her throat is slashed open and bleeding. *At least now you know what to look forward to.*

Fuck her. I turn so that I'm lying flat on my side, but my hair drips over the edge of the chaise, spilling onto the floor like blood. If I squint, that's what it looks like. Carnage. Death.

Murder...

He said she was stabbed. Did she even see it coming? Did she suffer?

I doubt it. Melanie *never* suffered the consequences of her actions. She wouldn't hesitate to put me or the others in her place, either.

So. She. Shouldn't. Matter.

God, I wish she was here. I'd punch her. Hit her. Say all those things I had enough tact not to while she was alive. I'd give her a real fucking sendoff.

She'd never have the last word...

And she still won't.

I shake my head as if the act alone can drive her out and rise from the chaise. Enough. She's dead.

She's *dead.*

Gritting my teeth, I escape into the bathroom and run the bath water as hot as I can stand it. The noise helps somewhat in drowning her out—but not completely.

I see her on the water's surface. She's smiling. Smirking, taunting me from the grave: *You call this struggling, sweetie? You've had it easy.*

Fuck her. Closing my eyes, I submerge myself beneath the water, counting the seconds.

One.

Two.

Ten.

Gasping, I resurface, only to find a stranger watching me from the mirror's surface. Her eyes are bloodshot. Straggly brown hair clings to her shoulders, a far cry from Melanie's multicolored wigs. But the haunted quality of their expression is the same.

Like mother like daughter...

I STARTLE to awareness in my room, blinking back the remnants of a nightmare. One of the shapeless phantoms chases me into the real world. When I leave my room, intending to make breakfast, he's standing at the base of the stairs.

Dressed in a gray suit, he takes one look at me and inclines his head. "Get dressed. I'll be waiting out front."

My fingers sneak to the inside of my wrist, pinching hard—but I don't wake up. "You're taking me?"

It's obvious. I think I just need to hear him say it.

His eyes sweep over me, revealing nothing. Turning on his heel, he approaches the door. "I'll be in the car."

Unease has me swallowing hard. Aware of him waiting, I wash up in record time and wrestle my hair into a ponytail. Minutes later, it is a surprisingly normal trip down to his car.

No dead mothers make an unwelcome appearance. No unspoken tension ruins the odd familiarity between us.

Hell, it could be just a normal day in Maxim Koslov's world —until I spot the uncharacteristic clutter lying across the car's front seat.

I'm stopped in my tracks, vaguely aware of the frown tugging on my mouth.

"One of the children must have left them behind last night," Maxim says, sounding miles away.

Them. Soft, red petals spill from a dying set of roses, tied together with white ribbon. They're cut short, the perfect length for placing on an altar.

Or a coffin.

I shake my head and wrench on the handle, opening the passenger's side door. "How... How was it?" The memorial service. God, just pairing that word in the same context with Melanie makes me snicker.

"It went well." He sounds so cold. I can't parse anything unspoken he might be hiding.

"G-good." With one hand, I grab the roses. Freeze. Their delicate scent taints the air and I can't help but picture Melanie. The artificial version was her signature stench— one so ingrained that it's like she's here, reeking of cheap, flowery cologne.

"I'll take those." Maxim snatches the roses from my grasp and tosses them onto the back seat. "Get in."

His voice sinks into my bones, jolting them into submission. I slump onto the passenger's seat, inhaling the air as shallowly as possible. I imagine my pores closing up in protest, refusing to absorb so much as a fucking ounce of him or the roses.

Breathe it in, baby, a woman's voice taunts, sounding so close that I swear I can smell cigarettes. *We might as well smell the same...*

"We're here."

I flinch, noticing our surroundings. Minutes must have passed without me realizing. *Here* is a parking lot surrounded by a lush, green lawn and towering stone buildings. I only have movies to compare this scenery to— one of those shitty thrillers taking place on a college campus. The lead female would be a beautiful, normal blond who grew up in a beautiful, normal family. Her tuition was paid for by a scholarship or some shit. Not by a man with seemingly more money than God.

She might be one of those bookish types too, who outsmarted the killer in the end and lived happily ever after. Such a good girl would never sell her soul to him in exchange for the kiss of his blade.

Sucks for her. To each his own.

"Your preliminary session is in that building over there," Maxim explains, nodding to a castle-like structure directly ahead. Without warning, he reaches across me and flicks the glove compartment open. "Here—" A new, glossy brochure lands on my lap, along with a slip of paper. "The room number is on it. I'll arrange for your transportation afterward."

"I can get home on my own—"

"I'm not going to hurt you." His stern glance makes me bite a retort back. He doesn't sound like the ruthless dominant demanding a concession. He won't hurt me.

Not intentionally, with whips or knives.

Supposedly not unintentionally, either.

"Fine." I swallow hard and wrestle for the handle. As I scramble for the curb, I find myself croaking, "B-bye."

His watchful gaze seers a hole through the back of my neck, tracking my every move across the deserted campus. At a second glance, this place holds little resemblance to the bustling college set from that movie. There are no students racing to their next class. No professors juggling books and supplies.

There is no one else *at all*.

Even inside the building, it's too quiet. The only other inhabitant I find lurks on the third floor, in a room marked 301—the same printed on the slip I'm holding.

The room itself is a narrow classroom with a view of a small, picturesque grove. Unlike in my movie—only one desk dominates a space obviously meant for many more. Across from it is a larger desk that I assume belongs to the professor. A woman is sitting behind it now, her blond hair neatly swept back into a bun. Spotting me, she stands up, tucking a piece of hair behind her ear. It's her most striking feature, considering that a beige dress and loafers barely distinguish her from the plain walls around us.

"You must be Francesca. I'm Gemma." She smiles, extending her hand. "It's nice to meet you."

"Likewise," I croak.

Her nails are manicured and pink, her skin flawless. No marks. No cuts. If anything, *she* resembles the bright-eyed protagonist from that fucking movie. Cast alongside her, I'd be the brunette slut who dies running from the killer in high heels.

"Shall we begin?" She nods to the empty desk, her hands folded primly over her lap. "This is more of a counseling session than anything. We'll go over a basic review first, and then you'll take the entrance exam. It's mainly to see where you place—"

"You're the professor?" The fact that she's a woman doesn't shock me. Knowing Maxim, I'm not surprised. But she's young. I'd peg her as only a few years older than I am, if that.

She's pretty too.

Not to mention that she doesn't exude the same twisted, business-like aura of Lucius or anyone else in Maxim's orbit.

As weird a term as it feels to use in this context, she's…*normal.*

"Think of me more as a private tutor," Gemma explains, her lips quirked in an amused grin. "Let's get started."

I perch myself on the smaller desk, placing the brochure in front of me. With all the gusto of some of my most eager high school teachers, Gemma directs me toward a set of review questions on the back page.

Ugh. Dread forms a knot in the pit of my stomach, tightening the longer I scan the assorted topics. Math. Science. Grammar. Each one triggers an unwelcome flashback to high school—the worst being the many fucking times a teacher would demand an answer to a question, but I'd be too damn tired to respond. Working the night shift wasn't conducive to learning, go figure.

"Let's start with some simple equations," Gemma suggests. "Think you can try this one?" She scribbles a series of numbers on the blackboard.

"I..." My brain stalls. In the end, I spout off a random number.

"Not quite," she says, tilting her head thoughtfully. "Let's look at it from another angle." She turns to the blackboard at the front of the room. Picking up a piece of chalk, she maps the problem out. "We can tackle it in pieces," she offers. Strange. I don't sense any mocking in her tone. Patiently, she guides me to the right answer and claps once I reach it. "Awesome! Now, let's try another."

A RED FUCKING pen can seem more menacing than a bullwhip or a leather belt in the right circumstances. With my final score in question, Gemma wields her tool as expertly as Maxim does his, manipulating it across my scrawled answers.

The final tally could lead to praise or potential punishment. Which one do I crave more?

My nails bite at my wrist in anxious nibbles. I can't decide on an answer.

"Relax," Gemma says, glancing up. Her eyes widen, honing in on my mouth. "Are you all right?"

I'm biting my lip. I don't realize that until warmth drips from my chin and seeps through the delicate collar of my dress. Absently, I swipe the substance from my neck. It's red.

"I-I'm fine," I say, rubbing my fingers along the side of my dress.

"Good, because I'm all done." Gemma presents my marked-up booklet to me and beams. "You passed. Good work."

"What?" My eyebrow shoots up into my hairline. "How?"

She laughs. "Don't sell yourself short. I'm going to recommend maybe some remedial English, but mainly for grammar."

"Maybe I should learn Russian while I'm at it," I blurt out. "I already know the word for kitten, anyway."

"Oh?" She inclines her head thoughtfully. "What is it? Though I'm afraid all I know is English."

A sharp, pinching sensation stabs through my stomach. "*Kotyonok.* That's the Russian term."

She shrugs. "I've never heard it before—" Then she breaks off suddenly, rising to her feet. Ivory displaces the pink in her cheeks, making her resemble that horror movie heroine even more.

The "murderer," I suspect, is standing in the doorway, casting a shadow that dampens the daylight streaming through the windows.

"I don't mean to interrupt," he says.

"I… We were just finishing up."

My stomach tenses, but I don't know why. She's startled— Maxim is certainly the type of man to inspire that reaction. I'm reminded of the first time I met him, how intimidating he seemed.

How intimidating he still is.

It's the odd hint of recognition that I find in Gemma's expression which confuses me. Obviously, they met before —he hired her. But there's more to it…

She stiffens, unconsciously brushing a hand along her throat, as if remembering a particular touch. The suffocating clench of someone's fingers.

His fingers.

Blinking, she shakes her head and forces a smile. "We're all done here. I'll do some research and then we'll discuss potential majors, Francesca." She's still smiling, but her cheery tone falls flat. Forced. Glancing beyond me, she nods. "It was good to see you, Mr. Koslov."

Maxim says nothing. Turning to face him, I'm not sure what I'll find. He's still wearing his suit from earlier, his hair slicked back instead of wild. Cold, his gaze is unreadable as ever. But...

I sense something lurking just beyond that stoic expression. Another revelation, maybe. Or another bombshell. About Melanie?

Or maybe *this*.

The curious reason why he brought me to be "tutored" by a woman he used to fuck.

CHAPTER ELEVEN

I've been in confined spaces with dangerous men before. Hell, thanks to Melanie, I've lived with them. Hid from them. Suffered at their hands.

Men who violated my life and my body in unforgivable ways—and I survived every last one. No matter what, I was always unbreakable, unshakable Frankie.

But this new monster...

He changed my name and invaded my soul. He turned me into a pet—a replacement. Simply one of a hundred.

"I could have enrolled on my own," I say, breaking the silence for the first time since we left the campus. "Found my own teacher. My own school—"

"Was Gemma not satisfactory?" The hard note in his voice makes me grit my teeth. It's defensive.

Around us, traffic flows smoothly, unaffected by the suffocating tension robbing the air from my lungs. For whatever reason, he's decided to drive himself again.

"She's nice," I admit, but that word has a hollow ring to it.

One he doesn't miss.

"You're wondering about my relationship with her." His eyes are on the road as he masters the steering wheel, his jaw clenched.

"I think I know." God, I sound so calm. Strange, when I feel anything but. My heart is trying to beat its way out of my chest, hammering against my throat in the process. "One of the women you referred to before?"

How did he put it? Women more beautiful than me.

Better than me.

"I was her client once, yes," he admits.

I wince, startled by the pain ripping through my wrist. I'm doing it to myself: scratching so hard that I break the skin.

"She came to me four years ago," he adds as if in afterthought. "But the position didn't suit her. I saw her potential in other avenues."

My brain takes that statement and runs with it, inferring what he doesn't say. The beautiful, scholarly Gemma came to him as a hooker, but he—good old Maxim—saw her *potential.*

"She couldn't do it?" I ask, staring at the streets racing past.

"No. She didn't belong. She voided the contract."

"Did…did you ask her why?" We're nearing the house. I sense the car pick up speed as it lunges through stoplights as if he can't wait to dump me there.

Still, he plays along.

"She needed money for her education. Her parents had declared bankruptcy, leaving her with a debt to pay." He almost sounds genuine. Like someone with an ounce of pity to spare. "Now, she has tenure at the university and knows a variety of subjects."

"You didn't call her *kotyonok,* did you?" I didn't mean to ask him that, but it's too late. Deep down, I already know the answer anyway. "She didn't know what it meant." Maybe all this time, I thought that name was a universal term he applied to all of his pets. But not her, Gemma. He calls her by name.

She was more than his wayward kitten—maybe they *all* were. The other women smart enough to leave him before he threw them aside like trash.

And that's all you are to him, baby. Melanie's voice slithers through my thoughts, tainting them. *Trash. Just like me. You think any man might feel differently? Think again.*

"You're upset, aren't you?" He phrases the statement as if doubting it the moment the words leave his mouth. "Look at me—"

"Goodbye, Mr. Koslov."

We're in front of the house now, parked in the driveway. A yellowish glow illuminates the windows; the kids are home. My lips twitch, fighting to remember how to smile as I reach for the door handle.

"No—" The car lurches backward and then veers onto the road so fast that I have to brace myself against the window.

Heart pounding, I look at him from the corner of my eye. He's rigid, hunched over the dashboard, his eyes on the blurring streets.

"What are you doing?" I ask.

"We're not done."

I can taste his anger, more potent than the perfume of those fucking roses.

"I asked you a question."

"Let me out," I rasp. But if he replies, I hear nothing. Just my pounding pulse and ragged breaths. One. Two. Ten. Fifty. The faster I inhale, the more lightheaded I feel.

He's zooming through traffic, running red lights...

With no fucks given, he veers across oncoming traffic and a barrage of honking horns deafen me as my stomach lurches to the back of my throat.

"Stop!" I tug at the handle, only to realize he's engaged the locks. "What are you doing?"

Seconds later, his high-rise seems to come from nowhere, looming above for a heartbeat before he turns into the garage. After he parks and switches the car off, I can breathe again.

"What are you doing?" I repeat, my voice shaking.

"Get out." He doesn't even face me before exiting the car. The door slams shut behind him, echoing like a gunshot. "We need to talk."

"I'm done talking."

So why aren't I running?

I'm copying him instead, approaching the elevator. Maybe I really am in that damn thriller. There's a monster on my trail, though he keeps his distance, calling out in a dangerously soft cadence.

"Did you hear me?" he wonders, his voice chasing me as I pull ahead of him.

Yes. I hear him. Just like I've heard a million others throughout my life. Teachers. Boys. Men. My mother. My sisters. My brothers.

You're too stupid to do anything but scrape, Frankie.

You have to take care of us, Frankie.

You're worthless, Frankie.

All you're good for is lying on your back...

"Look at me."

My spine curls at the lethality contained in just a few terse notes. Shit. There's no ignoring him. The entire elevator car crackles with tension, feeling impossibly small. Crushing myself in the corner can only buy me a second's reprieve. What the hell am I doing here?

I start for the closing doors and try to wedge my hand between them. "Take me back—"

"*Look at me.*"

A violent crack rips through the silence. The door slamming shut? No. His fist meeting the control panel so hard that a chunk of metal flies off and ricochets across the floor.

It misses me by mere inches, and I cringe, pressing myself against the wall out of instinct. But when I finally process my emotions, I only feel...pain.

Sharp and searing agony claws through my stomach, but my nails aren't the cause this time.

Poor baby, Melanie taunts. *You thought you were the special one? Ha!*

The room blurs, reducing Maxim to a golden blur on black canvas. No matter how hard or fast I blink, nothing holds the tears back.

"Are you bored?" I ask him. In the narrow space, I sound dangerously loud. "Is that why you brought me here? To fuck? To terrorize? Whatever it is, let's just get it over with." I claw at the front of my dress, undoing the buttons beneath the collar. *Ping!* They fly off one by one, dancing across the floor. "Should I bend over? S-stand? Just tell me where you want me—"

"Stop." He watches my pathetic performance without a shred of emotion.

"Here, then?" I'm already trying to shove my arms from the sleeves. "Just tell me—"

"Stop it." He's closer in an instant, grabbing me by my throat, clenching hard enough to cut off any sound I make.

I'm forced to stare up, but from this angle, his eyes burn. Like glimpses of hell smuggled in the gaze of an angel.

"Tell me what this is about," he demands.

"About?" I croak—the loudest reply I can force through his grip. None of this should be surprising. His real feelings shouldn't hurt. I should take his money like a good girl and perform whatever song he wants in return. "Just tell me how you want to use me. That's all I'm good for. Isn't it?"

He laughs, and never in my life has a sound ripped down my spine with such intensity, resonating in my bones. Like thunder, that first warning herald before one hell of a storm.

"I see it now. You're jealous." He lets me go and steps from the elevator, leading the way down the hall. "Of her," he calls back.

I should deny it. Shake my head.

Lie.

"Tell me," I choke out instead. "I just... I just need to hear you say it."

God, why do I sound so weak? Breathy. Desperate.

"Oh?" His tone rings with warning, begging me to heed it. *Stop this.*

Hell, every nerve in my body screams at me to do the same. *Get a hold of yourself, Frankie!* I bite my lip. Gouge at my wrist. Nothing clears my head. Instead, the same damn thought keeps echoing over and over. *Her potential. Her potential...*

"Was I that much of a whore?" I ask in a rush. I can't stop spitting each word out despite how his shoulders stiffen, his posture tenses. "Is that why you made your offer?"

Why you threw me away.

"Enough of this." He whirls on his heel without warning. His hand latches onto my skull, dragging me deeper inside.

I try to back away, but he's relentless, grasping me even tighter.

"Whore? Yes," he snarls. "Just like the rest. And to you, I was just a job. Look at me—" He tugs even harder when I try to turn away. Goosebumps swell over my skin, feeding off the tension radiating through him. It's like he's a fucking inferno—even though his voice chills me right to the fucking bone. "You want to know about *her?*"

He shoves me onto a leather chaise face down before I can reply. I twist my hips, fighting his grip—but his knee lands on my lower back, easily pinning me beneath him.

"The trembling little girl who came to me in a goddamn prom dress?" he hisses. "Who vomited on my cock before she could even take the damn thing in her mouth? A girl who wouldn't have lasted a day, let alone a night with me? And what about *you*?" He yanks my head upright, ripping tiny hairs from their follicle beds. My scream can't drown him out; he's that loud. "You came to me no better than she did. I showed you mercy. I told you to leave. You *disobeyed*—"

His voice rasps as if the concept confounds him, even now: I came back to him.

Again.

And again.

And again.

Suddenly, the pressure on my scalp loosens. Through streaming eyes, I watch him back toward the center of the room.

"I gave you what you wanted—more than all those fucking women combined." He's still shouting, straining the cords in his neck. I *feel* each bellowed word like he's hammering them into my skull. "Gemma has a husband. A child. The first time I spoke to her in four years was to request her services. For *you*. Fuck, the things I've done for you." He sounds awed. Disgusted. "The things I'm still doing. For *you*. Even when it costs me more than you can imagine. And you want to play this childish game? Like a mouse chasing the cat's tail. You enjoy this, don't you?" Amusement flickers across his expression, but it's mixed with something else, visible only in his stern frown. Something too heart-stopping to name. "Don't you?"

"Enjoy it?" I choke out. His madness is contagious. *I'm going mad.* I tear at my hair, rocking back and forth as the pain barely registers. "I hate it! Stop toying with my head. *You* threw me away—"

"Did I?" He glances around the massive room as if taking stock of each possession. The luxurious leather chaise. The polished, pristine floors.

And finally me, trembling at his mercy.

"Bored. You used that word. And I *should* be bored of you." He takes a step closer.

I jump back, but he advances again, another step. Another. His movements are jerky, devoid of the grace I'm used to. Almost as if he doesn't even realize he's doing it. Prowling. Hunting. Closing me in near the wall, eliminating my only escape route with a mere shift of his weight.

The second I flinch to the balls of my feet, it's already too late.

"You want to know about *kotyonok*—" His hand sweeps out, capturing a fistful of my hair again.

One ruthless yank makes me stagger into him, my hands grasping for leverage. I can feel his heart beating like this. It's fast. Unsteady. Manic. He doesn't care when I stiffen. His fingers just readjust their hold, crushing me against him.

"You were the only one whose name I didn't bother to learn at first. Just you," he admits, murmuring the confession into my hair. In a sick way, he sounds softer than before. Gentle. "You were right to be jealous. If you and Gemma both came to me that first day, I would have picked her."

Fire shoots through my chest. Is that pain? No, it's too sharp. Too raw. It doesn't numb me—it makes me reckless. "Get off of me!" I try to turn away, but his grip tightens.

"Don't." His teeth nip my earlobe as he snarls the warning. "I would have picked her," he echoes, an octave softer. "I could smell the desperation on you then. To you, I was a wallet. A job. A necessary evil. But I didn't judge you for that."

He doesn't sound angry. Merely crisp. Clinical. Like a scientist mulling his most puzzling experiment out loud, inviting anyone to offer insight.

"I knew you only wanted money. It's why I let you stay. It's why I didn't take the same pity on you that I did on the others. You were too young. And when you came back the first time…I knew exactly why. For money. And the second. And the third. All you wanted was fucking money."

He chuckles in that cold, chilling way, making goosebumps rise over my skin. We're too close. There's no escape from everything that makes him Maxim Koslov: the smell. The bulk. Those eyes glaring into my soul as if he knows everything I've ever tried to hide.

For what feels like an eternity, he stares into me. Through me. Whatever he finds just hardens his features further. He's stone within an instant, impossible to decipher.

"Believe it or not, I could stomach your greed. I have more than you've seen in your fucking lifetime. Enough to make you choke on it—" His free hand flinches for my throat as if he's intending to do just that. Choke me.

This time, for good.

Instead, he twists me around, shoving me face-first against the ice-cold wall. He's brutal. Unbearable pressure pins me in place: a prison made of flesh, and bone, and skin.

"It's not the money, is it?"

Warmth tickles the back of my neck: his mouth, nuzzling me. Biting me. Another gasp claws up my windpipe, but he's already licking the pain away before I can voice it.

"No... Something else keeps you coming back now."

There's no answer. None that I can give, and none that he'd believe. There's just silence, and a heartbeat—his and mine, hammering out a violent, unsteady rhythm in sync.

"I don't even think you know," he declares, sounding thoughtful again. "But it's wearing thin, Francesca... Though damn, maybe *this* is what you want?"

His fingers creep up my hips, groping through my thin clothing. Up my rib cage. To my breasts. The tighter he grips me, the more disjointed this moment feels. I'm in a parallel universe, where oxygen is an afterthought.

My body subsists only on *this*. His touch. His hate. Without warning, his nails sink into my skin. Lightly at first. Then firmer. Viciously. The tighter he holds, the harder I squeeze my eyes shut.

Harder. Harder. Light flashes before my eyes by the time he finally relents. Judging from the fiery welts stinging on my chest, he drew blood.

"I'm losing my patience," he admits, exhaling against my shoulder. "I'm losing my goddamn mind. Gemma, I could let her fuck someone else. She doesn't matter. I don't fucking care—but you?"

A shadow along the wall is my only warning before he wrenches my head to the side, baring my throat. A part of me lurches, anticipating teeth. Instead...I just feel the unstable gusts of his breath.

"I should bite you," he says against my skin. "Taste you. Make you bleed. More. Take all of you until there's nothing left."

He turns me around, capturing my throat in both hands, and yanking me onto the tips of my toes. Though my fingers fly out for stability, my nails catch the material of his jacket, accidentally seeking the flesh underneath. Bone.

He doesn't even flinch.

His hand cups my scalp, pulling me toward him, and I'm frozen. Blood. That's what we taste like as he forces his mouth to mine. Blood mingled together over bitten lips. Salt from my tears. Heat from his rage. Lust. Our tongues clash, his clambering to steal it all without sharing an ounce. And a terrifying thought starts to take hold: Maybe this is the only way I'll ever know how to let him in.

Through violence.

Because deep down, we're the same.

Selfish, twisted creatures.

CHAPTER TWELVE

J ust as quickly as the kiss began, he ends it, shoving me back. "Get on your knees." Each word crackles with barely concealed tension as he looms above, his hair obscuring part of his face.

I know the look in his eye, however, and I'm already staggering backward, rushing to obey the command. My knees strike the floor, bare beneath the hem of my dress.

I stare down at the bruised flesh, not looking up even as I hear him circle my position. My brain scrambles to take note of every nuanced emotion from him. He reeks of sweat and something else. Something sweet that drips from his fingers and taints the air like perfume.

"Your dress. Panties too," he grates out amid the telltale crunch of leather over fabric. His belt.

I picture it being wrenched from belt loop after belt loop. Impatiently. A shiver runs down my spine as I contort my arms behind my head and struggle to lift the fabric. The cool air kisses the bruises already there, but I barely feel the ache. By the time I rise onto my hands, the first crack of leather hits the air.

And the only thing I can do is *feel.*

He's reckless. A grunt rips from him with every brutal lash, mingling with the groans I barely manage to smother. In a twisted semblance of harmony, we create a symphony of muted agony and sadistic satisfaction. What feels like seconds later, it's over. His belt hits the floor with a thud, his breaths unsteady over the air.

"Get...up." His hand sinks into my hair, guiding my head back just enough so I can find him staring down on me, his eyes feral and unfocused. One hard yank and he has me on my feet, staggering down the hall, into his room, toward the bed.

I land on my back, my legs spread apart just enough for him to fit in between. He palms my waist, wrenching the hem of my dress up farther while pinning me flat against the mattress. With one hand, he reaches between my legs, cupping me in his palm.

I can't stifle a gasp. He feels hot. On fire. His fingers are slick as well, and I cringe as I wonder why—or maybe the moisture is from me? He hasn't touched me in days. I shouldn't crave that rough, bitter sting only he can deliver, but my hips are already arching into it, extending the torturous seconds.

"Still greedy," he bites out, stroking me with a callused finger. The anger is gone, and the teasing pinch on my clit is my reward. I think. He curls a thumb inside me before I can be sure, purposefully stroking my inner walls. "Roll over."

When I do, he smooths my hair along my back, guiding me upright. The other hand is still inside me, slowly churning my insides to mush.

"Your knees."

My thighs jerk apart, anticipating the moment he mounts the mattress behind me, his breath on my throat. Wet heat precedes the warning nip of his teeth. A tease. The next bite goes deeper, easily breaking the skin.

My lips fly apart, a moan caught between them. As if in punishment or encouragement, he bites down harder, tearing…grinding. My fingers sink into the sheets, straining the cotton. It isn't enough to anchor me though. My head floats, my thoughts drifting.

Clear. Crisp. Real.

"You're hungry for me. Aren't you?" Maxim growls into my ear, banishing the dark suspicions.

My body agrees with that assessment. Both nipples feel like razors teasing the inside of my dress. Each brush heightens the heat building in my blood. I'm starving, but he just might be poison and my body is torn between the risk of dying and the promise of instant gratification.

"Aren't you?" He nips me again, soothing the wound with a lick from his tongue.

The mattress sinks as he settles in behind me, throwing me off-balance. The hiss of a zipper being undone pierces the air, and then his fingers are between my legs again, nudging them further apart.

He breathes out after the first experimental thrust of his thumb. With the slightest bit of pressure on my clit, he has me lunging toward the headboard, bucking into his hand. He wields me like a tool this way, stroking and pinching to make me squirm. Make me scream.

Make me submit.

His broadness teases my entrance. Stretches me open. Wakes me up. My inner muscles clench, hungry for his length, but he doesn't thrust. He lingers, giving me the briefest taste of the fullness I crave.

It's maddening.

My legs shake, my fingers grasping for leverage. Just when I start to sway, he thrusts another half of an inch. Another. A burst of wetness coats him, easing his way—not that he takes advantage of it. It's like he's getting off from the anticipation of fucking me alone, thickening against my entrance. Driving me fucking insane.

Maybe this is his way of apologizing.

When he finally does thrust, it's a slow-burning chain reaction of friction and force. I'm on fire with every inch of me he claims, and I can't even tell how deep he really is when he slows and groans against my ear.

"You're shaking, *kotyonok*." Suspicion thickens his already guttural tone and snippets of fear mingle with pleasure.

He finds enough leverage to fist a chunk of my hair again, trapping me right where he wants me: back bowed, ass presented to him. When he pulls out, it's a sharp jerk of his hips that leaves me empty without warning. Not for long. I don't even have the chance to blink before the bed lurches and I'm full to bursting. I see white—he forces himself *that* deep. The feral grunt rumbling from his throat betrays his satisfaction. Control may get him off, but so does this: raw, primal fucking with a hint of restraint.

"Tell me why."

An answer I can't bite back springs to my lips. Lying is impossible when he's this close—dominating me. "A... Afraid."

"Why?" Confusion makes his voice shake. Makes *me* shake.

Another thrust, painfully slow. His free hand claws at my hip as if that much control is a struggle for him to achieve in this moment. He's straining at the seams again.

I wail as he lunges, sinking in so deep that I can't breathe. Pain. It paints the world black. It makes me desperate; I'm an addict itching for the only drug that gets her high. When he wrenches his grip, raising fire over my scalp, I'm thrown onto the dangerous precipice between sanity and clarity.

Can't think.

"Why?" he demands again.

The answer leaves me in a rush. "Because I shouldn't want you."

And I *do*. My body is a glove, gripping him so tight that I can feel every pulse of his cock. His chest heaves against my back as his mouth nudges my jaw. Within seconds, ravenous lips find mine. Crush them, battering me into submission. His tongue swipes. Invades. Subdues. It's not a kiss. It's a sampling. He'll devour me later, but like any predator, he toys with me first.

"Say it," he growls before nipping my bottom lip, eliciting a moan I can't smother. "What is it you want?"

Drugged on him, I can't lie.

"...to keep me," I gasp as my cheeks heat with shame. But there's more. *I want you to smother me. Capture me. Collar me. Break, break, breakbreakbreakbreakme.*

"Why?" he wonders, biting me harder when I don't answer.

Copper trickles between us and his tongue hungrily chases every last drop. I can't even feel disgusted. My body is on fire, aching on the devious edge of pain and fear. Horror and need. I feel like that fucking French queen, about to be beheaded, only I'm eager for the blade to come down. I *need* to feel it slicing me to pieces.

"Why?" Maxim questions for a second time, his voice colder. He's stopped moving, leaving me unbearably full, right on the edge of *real* insanity.

My brain stalls. "I…"

He shoves me down when I can't choke an answer out, flipping me onto my back. Cold silk rasps over my skin, alerting me to the fact that my dress is bunched around my waist. Only vaguely do I remember where we are. His bed.

And he doesn't seem to give a damn.

He takes my wrists in his hands, forming painful manacles out of his fists. Using his weight as a prison, he pins me down, grinding his pelvis just where I need him the most.

"I'm done toying with you, *kotyonok*," he hisses. At the same time, he thrusts, ramming his erection between my legs, aided by the teasing friction of cotton and silk.

It's torturous.

Desire curves my spine as my thoughts meld into one overriding sentiment: *Holy fuck*. My limbs liquefy. My breath catches. Just as the pleasure scrapes me raw, his nails gouge my inner wrists and the pain bites deeper, keeping me tethered to my body. To him.

"You want to be kept," he reiterates, still crouched above me. "Why?"

"I…" Another brutal assault centered near my clit stimulates my nerves into painful awareness. My lips part, spitting out words at his command before I can properly compose them. "Because...feel...with you."

"Again," Maxim snarls against my throat. Shock doesn't color his tone. Just impatience. God, it's like he's in my head, seeing what I can't, ripping me apart to seek out the secrets I thought I was so good at keeping. "Say it." Pinching teeth startle me into obedience.

"Feel," I breathe. "You make me feel."

The Frankie Marconi I know and hate would never utter those words. She'd never whimper them while twisting her hips for another hint of agonizing ecstasy. She'd never fucking mean them.

And Maxim would never push her like this. Punish like this.

"How?" He thrusts his hips again, taking another moan from me.

He's different with this woman who's so eager to be his doll. He's reckless with her.

Bruised and battered, she'll never fucking forget who she belongs to. He'll handle her roughly and glue her broken parts together.

The worst part? She'll be grateful for every new crack.

My thoughts form the words more quickly than my tongue can push them out. "Something. Anything..."

Maxim laughs, swallowing my words with a bruising pass of his lips, and I have no doubt that he will make me regret every word.

He'll make me regret every twisted minute I continue to play his game.

And I'll never feel more fucking alive.

Bound to him, I won't have a damn choice…

And maybe the promise of that oblivion is what I really wanted all along.

I let myself sink into the brutality of his kiss and the violence promised within every harsh brush of his lips. His fingers bite into my ass, yanking me closer with our mouths still fused.

Rather than slow, he rocks his hips, slamming into me. Again. And again. And again… Heat builds, even though I don't want to acknowledge it. Sore flesh melts beneath his assault. Nerves spark. Catch fire. The air in my chest becomes liquid. My thoughts are smoke.

He's an inferno.

Gritting his teeth, he holds nothing back. Two thick fingers sink between my legs and find my clit, grinding the bundle of nerves into fucking oblivion. Stars. Tension. *Fuck!*

It isn't an orgasm that rips through my body—it's an entirely new reality. Sweat and skin become my universe. Everything else ceases to matter.

Breathless and spent, I watch him finish seconds after I do. His hands grip the headboard on either side of me, his head rearing back. Guttural, broken noise rips from his chest: a demon's growl. It reverberates through marble and chilled air. Seconds later, his release floods me, dripping down my thigh as he abruptly pulls out.

He's still hard somehow. Like a battering ram, he nudges my inner thigh, painting me in streaks of cum and sweat.

I WAKE up with three fingers inside me. Twisting, curling, maddening fingers. They swirl along my inner walls, drawing a cry from my throat. It's promptly swallowed by the warm surface that nudges my mouth open. *Lips?* I don't have any time to be sure before I'm consumed. Deep, hungry pulses of a tongue push me further to the edge. *Off* of it.

I'm clenching, swipe by swipe like a windup toy. Before my thoughts can reassemble, they're scattering apart toward different sides of the room.

"Look at me."

My eyes fly open on command and I find the devil hovering above. His black eyes trace my own, which watch on in satisfaction as they glaze over and then roll into the back of my head. *Shit.* My back bows, and my lips stretch around a moan.

The physical pleasure is maddening. But when his free hand latches onto my hip, his nails sinking deep...

Explosions. He rips me to pieces, melds them all back together, and calls it a "climax."

My body protests as he eases his fingers from me. Already, he's reaching for his cock, stroking his hand along the rigid shaft. He runs the crown along the length of me. The first thrust stretches me wide. The next, he's in to the hilt.

His name rips from my throat, hoarse and broken. It's the only coherent word I can manage, and for the moment at least, it seems to be enough. He growls in satisfaction at the sound, rolling his hips as he fucks into me. Thrust after thrust after thrust...

I'm mindless. My thoughts consist of an endless loop of only one word: *Shit...shitshitshit!*

It feels like an eternity before he finally comes, lunging against me—*into* me. Seconds later, he's rolling away, leaving my body naked on his bed.

His bed. It feels important to drill that point home. These sheets reek of him; the mattress has conformed to his body's imprint. But I'm the only woman to ever lie on it—I know that terrible truth without even having to ask. The walls inhale our combined scent, tossing it back at me like a flashing neon sign.

You're the only bitch who's been fucked here.

I'm the only bitch dumb enough to stay. I have to dwell on that fact as my blurred vision focuses on the ceiling. I blink twice to clear it, enough to make out his shadow pacing in the center of the room.

He frowns, looking me over. His jaw is clenched, those eyes like midnight. Anger is a familiar expression on him, but even that doesn't come close to describing this one. It's an unknown characteristic to his features, more terrifying than rage.

"I called you *kotyonok* because from the second you came to me you were on your guard, ready to pounce. Ready to bite." Still pacing, he frowns, raking his hand through his hair as if rearranging his thoughts. He's been thinking about this, I realize. "The other women were hardened. Most of them. Even Gemma knew what to expect. But you? So eager for your reward, you didn't even read the rules." He chuckles at that, grating the sound off his teeth. "Few lasted a night. Fewer an entire day. As I have told you before, you are the only one to stay. Contract or otherwise…you are the only one to stay."

He lets it sink in. Before, he was vaguer in his generalizations. He never came right out and told me that I was the only one. Or maybe he did. Maybe it was easier to ignore him then, in the cold, lifeless cage of the suite— before he showed me parts of himself that had been previously off-limits. Before he waltzed right into my home and made a mark on my family.

Maybe, in his own way, Maxim even tried to warn me.

"I told you," he says as if reading my mind again, consuming my thoughts the same way he has everything else. "Coming back to me was your first mistake."

"And the s-second?" My heart plays a pathetic pitter-patter pattern against the inside of my chest. I don't want to hear the answer, but my ears won't shut. My hands don't move to cover them, either. I'm at his mercy.

Where you belong, a part of me taunts. *Where you want to be...*

Maxim sighs as his footsteps slow. "You came," he admits. "Around me. For me." The raspy note in his voice makes the tiny hairs along my arms stand on end. "I told you that no one ever has. I *told* you." I know what he really means: *I warned you.* "But even that was a forgivable offense. Do you want to know what the final nail in your coffin was, *kotyonok*?"

"What?" I whisper, fighting for air as my heart swells, squeezing the breath from my lungs.

He sighs. "I don't think you'd understand, even if I told you."

He advances on the bed, climbing onto the mattress before I can blink. His hand cinches my waist, dragging me toward him.

"Sleep," he commands near my ear. "Tomorrow... Tomorrow we will talk."

CHAPTER THIRTEEN

"He's baiting me. No. I'll let him play his game." Nearby whispers meld into a deafening hum as snatches of reality gnaw away at my psyche.

And then it hits me. I'm in *his* suite. In his bed. His bite marks are on my neck.

And his words are in my head: *I don't think you'd understand, even if I told you.*

No. I shake my head to banish the thought, but the motion only betrays me.

"I'll handle it later." The murmured voices trail off and footsteps advance in my direction. Finally, a man commands, "Get up."

I peel my eyes open and witness his face in the dim glow of a nearby lamp. God, he truly resembles the devil. His eyes gleam red, his expression fierce, his lips glistening. There is something clenched in his fist.

Without warning, he throws it at me: soft, silky fabric that rasps over my naked skin. "Put it on. Then meet me out front." Then he's gone before my eyes even fully adjust and dread sets in.

Talk, he said—but my brain comes up with another word for it: regress. We'll meet in another secluded diner. He'll take back all the things he said.

And I'll be tossed in the trash again.

For a second—just one—I toy with the idea of running. Leaving him there and letting the master with all the cards know what it's like to be left holding a shitty hand.

Then logic takes over. Groaning, I pull myself upright and creep down the deserted hallway, entering "my" room for the first time in what feels like an eternity. I wash up quickly and stagger to the closet before I remember that I've already been given my costume.

The dress is black, I realize once I return to his room and fish it from the twisted sheets on the bed. It's low cut but relatively modest. After grabbing a pair of heels from my closet, I leave the suite and take the stairs down to the first floor. His car is idling out front, but this time, the driver is occupying the front seat and Maxim is dominating the back.

Upon spotting me, he wrenches the door open from the inside and beckons me with a wave of his hand. It's earlier than I thought. The sky is a coal-colored shade of gray and darkness floods the car's interior as I climb inside and close the door behind me.

My eyes dart toward him, but his face reveals nothing. He stares forward as the driver navigates toward a destination he and the driver must have already discussed between them.

Minutes later, we arrive before the elegant mansion I recognize as his club.

"Come."

Darkness still spreads across the sky as he unfurls himself from the car, rising like a goddamn giant. He's wearing a suit, black and crisp. It accentuates his muscles as he starts past me, advancing toward the entrance to the club.

I follow, partly unnerved, partly enthralled.

It's unfair how beautiful he can seem like this. With his hair wild and slicked back, his posture blazing confidence.

I'm not the only one entranced by him, either. A hush falls over the club as we enter. It's packed to the brim with its usual blend of scantily clad women, powerful-looking men, and pulsing music. Maybe he'll do it here?

Cut me loose and then choose another woman from this harem.

I tense as he slows his pace. Just when I start to suspect the worst, he turns in a different direction, ignoring the main club entirely. I'm not sure where he's heading, just that we pass through swatches of people before all other sounds finally die down.

We're in a hallway. He travels down to the very end and disappears through a doorway. When I finally gather up the strength to follow him, the air leaves my lungs.

It's a bedroom, I think. At the same time, it's so much more. His room back at the suite, if it could even be called that, is a crypt—detached of all semblance that it could have ever been inhabited by a human being. This room though...

It's bigger, for one, but it seems more cramped somehow. Lived in. The walls are that iconic shade of black, the floors marble. A minibar dominates one end of the room, and stone dust streaks the floor, leading to a section of the wall where a row of finished statues gleam in the glow of a silver light fixture. Most of them are abstract figures, with a few recognizable shapes sprinkled throughout: a wolf's head, a doe's, a woman's. *One* woman. Her face appears a few times, her features similar: a plain face with a simple nose and empty eyes without pupils. She's always naked. Always contorted into some unnatural position: her arms reaching toward something that isn't there.

If I squint, she almost looks familiar...

Turning away, I focus my attention on anything else.

At the center of the room is the strangest sight of all: a massive bed, the blankets rumpled, the pillows disorderly. My nostrils instinctively flare, but I only sense one scent.

Musk and sweat. Maxim. No one else comes into this room, I suspect.

Not even to clean. Never to fuck.

It's *his.*

My heart pounds as he crosses the threshold and nudges the door closed. That quiet thud shoots through me like a gunshot. I feel like I'm breaching the sanctity of this place. An intruder.

Apparently, the suite is just a temporary rest stop. *This* is where he lives.

It's like he realizes it too, once he sees me here, occupying a space I don't think he's let anyone else invade. Which is funny, given that more people probably run in and out of this club than I care to imagine. The fact that he can commandeer something so private speaks to the power he carries over this place. Over people.

A hint of it lurks in his muscles as he draws back and observes me. "We are going to play a game."

He gestures to a small table I didn't notice before, tucked into a corner of the room. It's black, and on it is a pack of cards with glossy, ebony backings.

"A game," I echo, creeping as close as I dare. The more I twist the prospect around in my brain, the more horrifying it seems. I don't think he plans on playing Go Fish. "A card game?"

A rare smile quirks his lower lip, gone in a second. "It's something one of my associates dreamt up. A bit childish, but for now, it will serve my purpose."

What purpose, exactly? I wait, my heart in my throat, but he doesn't say. Instead, his eyes flick over me, narrowing as they take me in.

"Sit."

I obey in a mass of trembling limbs. My muscles throb. Everything aches. My thoughts are way too clear. I'm aware of *everything.*

His nearness. My thudding pulse. More than that, even. Like the subtle way his breathing changes once I look up and meet his gaze. He's panting, inhaling my unease. Getting high off every drop, I suspect.

"Look." He takes the seat across from me and lifts the deck. One by one, he lays an array of cards face up. For some reason, I expect the typical arrangement: kings, queens, hearts, clubs, etc.

I shouldn't be so damn surprised by the designs I find printed on each card instead. One sports a bloodied heart in vivid detail. Another displays what I think is a flogger, with tiny metal beads dangling from the ends of it. There's also a pair of handcuffs, and a whip, and—of course—a knife.

"The game is simple," Maxim says while cutting the deck in half. He places one stack before me and keeps the other for himself. "You draw a card and I will guess which one it is. You do the same to me."

I lick my lips. It sounds so fucking simple, but nothing ever is where he's concerned. "And if I lose?"

His eyes flash, displaying a fleeting emotion that disappears before I can name it. "If you fail, I decide your punishment."

He waits, almost daring me to ask, *And if I win?*

He shrugs. "You do the same."

Again, it sounds too easy. "How am I supposed to—"

"Draw," he commands, nodding to the cards on my end. "I will guess first."

My fingers shake as I brush them over the topmost card. Slowly, I flip it over, concealing my selection from him: a whip.

He eyes me for so long that I start to wonder what the real purpose of this "game" is. To unnerve me, obviously. To make me sweat and squirm. To keep me guessing, even if he's supposedly the one in the hot seat, trying to decipher me.

"You drew a whip," he says finally. When I gasp, he clarifies, "You look too eager."

Eager. I marvel at that even as my stomach twists into uneasy knots.

"For your punishment, you give me an answer." He shifts slightly in his seat, leaning forward, his hands braced over the polished wood of the table. "How long do you see yourself staying with me, should I rescind my other offer?"

In other words: *If I dust you off and pluck you from the trash, how long before I toss you aside again?*

An answer springs to my lips almost too quickly. "A month, maybe."

He frowns. I answered wrong.

"Guess," he snaps while fishing a card from his own deck. Coldly, his eyes scan the surface, impossible to read and unbearable to decipher.

Seconds tick past before I give up with a halfhearted guess. "A knife?"

"No." He flips his card over: another whip. "I win again." Lifting the card, he observes it in the dim lighting. Then he places it apart from the rest. "Your punishment."

A shiver runs down my spine. I can't breathe. Only sheer force of habit makes me obey when he commands me, "Draw."

I do, but my eyes barely register the object on the other side of the card before he says, "A knife."

"How?"

"You are easy to read when it comes to the things that excite you."

My heart skips a beat. Excite?

He doesn't elaborate. Instead, he reaches out and snatches the card from my grip. Laying it beside the whip, he sighs. "I win again."

And I've supposedly earned my next punishment. I eye the knife warily as he draws another card. When I scan his face, however, something itches across my skull. Recognition? I know this expression.

I blurt out a guess without even thinking it through. "A heart."

He stiffens. Then, very carefully, he flips the card over, revealing the image printed on it.

"I win," I rasp in shock.

But beating him was the easy part.

His eyes meet mine again, more piercing than before. "And my punishment?"

Only he can make something so harmless—a childish game —seem so damn serious.

"The truth," I demand. "Why did you throw me away?"

He sits back, running his fingers along his chin. I'm caught off guard by how casual he makes the act appear. Almost like he planned for things to end like this all along. When his eyes flicker knowingly, I'm sure of it.

This whole game was an elaborate ploy for this: He needed a reason to talk. And a way to ensure I was ready to listen.

"You see yourself staying with me for a month," he says, twisting my words against me. "But maybe that would be for the best. Because being with me. *Truly* being with me... You would be risking way more than an occasional injury. In my world, you do not *keep* anything you're not willing to kill for. Money. Power. Prestige. You must be willing to lay your life down for it all. But a woman?"

He looks down, eyeing the table as if it offends him. Clenching a fist, he sets it down over the image of the heart, blocking it from sight. "My own father couldn't provide that protection to my mother. She was cattle. Do you understand what I mean?"

No. My brain isn't deranged enough to imagine exactly what he's implying—but it comes close.

"His own brothers could touch her," he says, confirming the worst. "Hit her. Abuse her. And he would let them. Why?" He lifts his shoulder in a heartless shrug. "Because to defend her with his life would mean defending her from *them* and he was too selfish, even though he plied her with lies of love and affection. My methods may seem harsh, but when a contract is terminated, there are no loose ends. No possession to protect."

"So...if they thought you cared for me—" My voice breaks. Even suggesting it seems unnatural. "You think they might hurt me."

"I *know* they would."

My stomach churns. I feel sick. "And you'd let them? You'd let them do those things to me?"

He doesn't say anything.

Sweat creeps across my palms as I reach for my deck and peel another card from the top. Without fanfare, I flip it over and slam it onto the table. How fitting. Another knife, just like the figurative one I feel twisting in my chest.

"So why even bring me here?" I demand, blinking rapidly. I won't... I am. Tears spill down like acid, eating through my skin. "You want to keep the stupid contract? Fine. But why do you keep toying with my head—"

"Because I can't let you go." He raises his fist and slams it over the heart. Once. Twice. With each blow, the entire table shakes. "I won't. And I should. That motherfucker is already asking about you."

My brain stalls. Sevastyn?

"I don't...I don't understand—"

"If he touches you, I'll kill him," he growls. "But I *can't*." He unfurls his fists and upends the entire table. *Bam!* It slams to the floor halfway across the room and every card goes flying. A flicker of shadow from the corner of my eye is my only warning before his hand captures my chin. "If I kill him. I'm done. Everything I've worked for. Everything I've slaved for. Gone. Are you really worth so much? Though, fuck, maybe it's not even *you* I want, either?" Laughing, he shakes his head, sending golden hair falling across his shoulders.

The locks obscure his face. Good. I can't even imagine an expression to match the grit in his voice. He's thinking out loud—and that's the terrifying part. Nothing unnerves me more than the brief glimpses I've had inside his mind.

"Maybe it's the idea of it," he says through gritted teeth. "The idea of having someone to fuck when I want. Hurt however I can. Someone foolish enough to stay so that I don't have to constantly look for someone new. That could be it…"

Frozen solid, I'm a slave to his touch, interpreting every fucking detail that I can from his coarse fingertips. They graze my skin, a heart-stopping caress. Eventually, he cuts my reprieve short, tilting my head back, forcing me to meet his gaze directly.

Dark, swollen irises convey so much in one glance. I can't interpret it all. Just that I'm in danger. Horrible, lethal danger.

And not because he might choke me.

Because he's confused. He's thinking. Without ever giving me the fucking chance to have any input, he comes to a decision within seconds. Like a door slamming shut, his expression shifts into a hardened mask.

"Could you stay, then?" he wonders. "With no contract? No promise of protection?"

And, if he were the kind of man to even offer such a thing, no love.

I know what he wants me to say—what I should say.

Of course not.

"My own mother didn't want me," I hear myself argue instead. God, I sound so old, aged a million years in just a few goddamn seconds. "I'm used to rejection. Hell, maybe I don't want you, either—"

"Don't lie to me."

I flinch as he shifts his stance and drops to his knees. With his height, it's easy for him to block me in. I brace for an assault, but his forehead meets mine without malice, his breaths scalding my cheek.

And this is worse than violence.

"Not now. Don't fucking lie to me. I wish it were just the sex." He laughs. Growls. "Any other man could fuck you. Keep you. But you haven't seen a client a fraction as often as you've been with me—this unnerves you. Any other woman could give me her body for a price. But no..." His fingers sink into my hair, gathering strands of it in a brutal fist. "It's *your* skin. My marks on it," he hisses near my ear. "Your scent. The way you move. Your fucking voice—" He tugs and stands, hauling me to my feet as well. Trapped by his bulk, I'm crushed against the wall, forced to endure every word of his confession. "It's you. And *you* threaten everything I've built. Everything I've worked for... But I can't let you go."

"Then don't." My face is buried against his chest and I pray that the cotton of his suit muffles every fucking word.

Because once I've started, I can't seem to stop. "I just want…"

"What?" he demands.

"To submit," I say in a rush. "*One* aspect of my life when someone else takes complete control of everything for once. Someone who won't throw me out or push me away. I don't care about the rest. I just want to *stay*."

My nails dig into the fabric, biting into the tender flesh beneath to convey what I can't put into words.

"It's out in the open now," he says, his voice rough. Strong hands grip my waist, bunching up the skirt of my dress. "You know my limits. I've hidden nothing."

His limits: I'll never be worth fighting for. His club. This room. His world. All of it takes precedence over me.

Can I live, knowing that?

His lips brush my jaw before I can decide and every thought vanishes. "Everything else I can give you," he swears. "Money? Fine. However fucking much you want. An education? A home for your family? I'll give you that."

And all of it tethered to a contract, nothing more.

Which is fine. I don't need anything else. I tell myself that over and over as his teeth nip at my lower lip, pry my mouth open, and claim every inch for himself.

I tell myself that as he backs me to his bed and crushes me to the broken-in mattress.

I chant those fucking words: *Material things are all I need.*

Maybe if I repeat it enough times…

I'll finally believe it.

"Get up."

The husky voice, paired with a fiery splash of pain on my hip, draws me from a dreamless, heavy sleep. Peeling my eyes open, I find Maxim sitting beside me, his palm hovering over my smarting skin, ready to strike again.

"Come."

I crawl after him to the end of the mattress, groaning in a mixture of pain and exhaustion. It has to be some time in the afternoon, judging from the sliver of sunlight seeping beneath the black curtains that shield the windows. He's kept me here for hours.

Was this part of my punishment? Getting fucked into oblivion?

I bite my lip as a pang shoots through my belly. It wasn't hope. It *wasn't.*

"Come here."

He leads me into a nearby bathroom. Gold fixtures and white marble are a chilling contrast to the darkness of his room. After steering me into a sunken tub, he runs the water hot and watches as the liquid rises, lapping at my skin.

Looking down, I don't even recognize myself. A patchwork of cuts and bruises stand out in brutal contrast to pale skin. Only now can I feel the sting and ache from each little injury. My left eye throbs the most.

"Don't—" He stops me from reaching up to touch it, capturing my wrist.

I can't breathe as he lowers my hand to the water and then flicks his thumb along my cheek instead.

"When I sculpt, every strike must be precise. Controlled," he says gruffly, observing my wound like he would a cracked bit of marble. "The slightest chip can often be smoothed or polished—but a crack is irreparable. I can only start over, move onto something else. But *this*..." He lightly teases his nail against my skin, just enough to bite. "I can't start over new."

His jaw clenches in the dangerous way it does when he's thinking. Contemplating. Plotting.

"I suggest another game," he says, lowering his hand. When I stiffen, he shakes his head. "Not like that. This one... If I ever hurt you again, you have my permission."

I'm cold despite the steam wafting from the water around me. It's up to my chest now, and the gentle flow from the faucet adds a haunting backdrop to his low, careful tone.

Hurt. He doesn't mean via the lash of the whip or the sting of his blade during foreplay.

"Permission to what?" I croak when seconds pass without an explanation.

His fingers leave my hair and move to my hip, this time with a washrag caught between them. "Permission to render your own punishment," he says. "I will give you that."

Shock lances through me. Punish him how? I'm not brave enough to ask. His promise lingers, tainting the air as he washes me up in earnest.

There is no rose-scented soap here. Instead, he lathers me with a scent that smells like him. Musky, spicy, and masculine. I don't know how long he bathes me in total— just that he takes his time, extending every touch and caress.

I wouldn't call it gentle. More resigned. The same way the drug dealers in my old neighborhood used to wash their expensive cars out in the open, daring anyone to touch their property. As the water drains from the tub, he disappears, slipping into the hallway, and I finally let myself process the snippets of what happened last night.

So much about his bipolar mood makes sense now—and that's the fucking terrifying part. He makes perfect sense. I can easily guess what will happen next. For now, he'll keep me around, but the moment I get too close. Push him too far. Draw too much attention from his fucked-up family.

He'll cut me loose again.

"Lift your arms," Maxim commands, snapping me back to the present.

He got a dress for me while I was lost in thought. With little fanfare, he redresses me in the black shift I wore here. Together, we return to the now deserted main hall of the club and then out front, where his driver awaits.

It's only when we're halfway across the city that I stop to consider how dangerous this game of roulette has become. It's one thing when the bullet is an unknown number of pulls on the trigger away. It's another entirely when the bullet is in your goddamn hand.

Safety. Security. Sex. I've bled for those things before. But maybe that's the point. Who am I *without* the constant, soul-numbing struggle I've known my entire life?

That's the real question.

HE TAKES me home and I find the kids in the living room. Dread weighs me down as I linger in the foyer, listening to their laughter drift through the doorway. This time of day, I can't scurry past them or hide from sight.

Inhaling, I start forward, taking stock of the battlefield before me. Ainsley and Eric are trying to stab each other with the ends of expensive-looking fake flowers while Mikie and the boys shout at the television, game controllers in hand. I spot Daisy lurking into the shadows. The moment I enter the room, she's already sneaking out before I can say a word.

Sighing, I start after her. "Daisy, wait—"

"She's okay," Mikie says without looking away from his game. "Give her some time to cool off… You look like shit." His eyes sweep over my damp hair and my wrinkled dress. "Sorry," he says a second later. "I just meant—I mean. Hey."

"Hey," I choke out.

Ainsley and Eric are watching me, frozen mid-fight. Ollie and Ray stare too, while Mikie turns back to their game, his shoulders hunched.

I don't know what else to say other than, "How…how are you guys holding up?" The neckline of this dress is too damn low. Awkwardly, I cross my arms over my chest in a pathetic attempt to disguise the bared flesh. "Everything okay?"

"Fine," the twins say in unison.

"Fine," chirp Eric and Ainsley.

Mikie sets his controller down. "We're all good," he says, flashing a crooked grin. His eyes meet mine, unusually sharp. He's trying to tell me something, but he doesn't say what out loud—for their benefit, I realize.

Then it hits me, a figurative punch to the chest: He's playing the role I used to, keeping the kids calm while the deadbeat mother makes her occasional appearance.

"Get back to the game, you dummies," he barks to Ollie and Ray. "Let's see how many times I can kick your asses!"

I back out of the room, heading for the stairs. My eyes sting. My throat is on fire, but this time, I'm not sure why.

Relief? They're doing fine without Melanie.

Or me—which is a good thing...

"The police were here again, you know."

I look up and find Daisy standing at the top of the steps, her arms crossed, her pink lips in a flat line. I don't even recognize her voice, so dull that she might as well be whispering.

"That bald guy scared them off. But they said some stuff."

"What?" My heart races, my palms slick. "What did they say?"

"That guy Mama married is dead too. Did you know that?"

My eyes widen before I can school my expression. "No," I rasp. "I didn't."

"He is." She squares her jaw, something she does only when she's upset but trying to save face. A trait she picked up from me. "The police said he was in a gang. They said more stuff, too."

"Like what?" I reach out, grasping the banister for support. The walls are spinning. The spacious house feels too damn small, like the foundation might crack beneath the pressure.

"They asked if you and Mama had a fight."

"Oh." I struggle to keep my voice even. "And what did you say?"

"The truth." Her eyes gleam, harder than I've ever seen them. Then, without a word, she turns and disappears down the opposite end of the hall.

"Daisy, wait!"

I mount the rest of the stairs, but I don't follow her. It's only when I'm in the room designated as my own that I finally notice something tucked into the folds of my dress like an afterthought. It's stuck to the fabric—a black card sporting the image of a bloody, beating heart.

I stare at it as my eyes water and burn. Gasping, I bring my opposite hand to my mouth and bite down so hard that I taste salt.

Of all the things a billionaire psychopath can promise to give me, he keeps the most dangerous item of all for himself.

But at least he has control of his—my heart is in six pieces with nothing left to share for anyone else.

No matter what price he'd be willing to pay.

CHAPTER FOURTEEN

He gives me one night with my family. One miserable night spent hiding in my room while the sounds of their laughter drift up through the floor.

The next morning, Lucius is waiting for me before the kids even leave for school. Rather than to the suite, he brings me to the college and another lesson with Gemma passes in relative normalcy.

Whatever that means.

"You did good," she says when our time is up. I don't miss how her eyes cut up to my bruised, ravaged neck. "Take care, Francesca."

A black car is waiting for me out front of the building, driven by a man whose gaze meets mine through the windshield. *Zap!* It's like I spent the entire day sleepwalking —now, I'm awake, electrified into awareness.

Clarity paints Maxim Koslov in terrifying detail as he exits the car and circles around to my end while I approach. He opens the door to the passenger's seat, but the look in his eye raises the hairs on the back of my neck.

It's determined.

"Get in," he tells me.

I swallow hard as I perch myself on the leather seat and he closes the door behind me. Five seconds are my only reprieve before he re-enters the car on the driver's side. Palming the steering wheel, he sighs.

"You are going to stay with me tonight." Gritting his teeth, he shakes his head and tries again. "I...I want you to stay with me tonight."

My breath catches inside my lungs. I'm suffocating even as my brain desperately tries to process his question. Our new understanding demands new rules, apparently.

It's not enough for him to command, or for me to obey.

I have a choice this time.

Choose to play the game despite knowing how it'll inevitably end.

"*Kotyonok*," he prods when my silence stretches too long. Tension coils his posture, and his knuckles are white.

"Okay," I rasp in response. "Okay."

When the car comes to a stop, we aren't in front of the house. Or his suite. A tall brick building looms above. A window framed in dark-colored drapes displays an empty dining room, the sight of which raises goosebumps over my arms.

Once we pass through the main doors and a smiling hostess rushes to meet us, I remember. *This* is the place where we first went over the terms of his contract. In bloody thorough detail.

I can't suppress a shiver as we're led toward that exact same table. It's set for two, the silverware flickering a dangerous, burnished gleam.

"Have a seat, *kotyonok*," Maxim commands.

He's already seated, his eyes tracing my body. He's wearing gray today, matching my outfit either by accident or intention. The color brings out the harshness to his features in a way black or white never could. He's beautiful, polished stone, set with eyes of obsidian that warn anyone caught in their glare not to disobey.

I stagger toward the empty chair and collapse onto it, scooting in as close to the table as I dare. The moment our gazes reconnect, Maxim reaches under the table and withdraws an item that must have been in his pocket: a folded slip of paper. Without explanation, he rips the document in half and then slides both torn ends toward me.

"Our previous agreement," he tells me, his eyes fixated on mine as if hunting my reaction down. At the same time, he grabs a bottle from the table and pours a layer of scarlet liquid into a glass on his end. Without a word, he does the same to a glass near me.

My fingers jerk against the white tablecloth. I almost can't control the need to reach for the torn contract and press those broken pieces back together. Memorize that monetary amount and cling to it like a fucking prayer.

"So, now?" I force myself to ask, my voice faint. "What happens next?"

A lethal smile quirks his lower lip. Or maybe it's a frown, exasperated and terse. "When I do business, I never renege on my terms." He's not referring to the shadowy dealings of his empire. Oh no, his tone is too guttural. "I know what I want from the outset. Always. I never want more. Now?" He nods to the glass beside my trembling hand, a silent command to drink.

I do, choking down a single sip. If his aim was to help relax me, it backfires. My throat is a fucking desert. Swallowing doesn't ease the dryness at all. "I don't know what you mean."

"This is an unusual situation," he admits, sounding partly amused and partly...not. "I don't make a habit of discussing my intentions with someone like you."

"Well, I don't make a habit out of sleeping with criminal billionaires." My cheeks flame when I realize how fucking bold that sounds out loud.

Even more insane? He doesn't look insulted.

"Criminal?" His eyes flash, his tongue tracing his lower lip. It's like he tastes the word, melding it with his next sip of wine. "And what might give you that impression?"

I can't tell if he's joking or not, but his stern expression demands a response. "You kill people."

He laughs. "Am I so obvious?"

He *is* joking. My heart lurches as my thoughts stall. Reacting to him should be harder than this. "No," I finally say. "I'm just not as naïve as I pretend to be."

"Like your sister? *Don't*," he warns as my heart sinks through the goddamn floor.

My fingers grip the table, and it takes everything I have to stay seated. So this is what he meant by "discussing my intentions."

"I won't hurt her. But I must say, she is very perceptive."

"What did she say?" God, I can't breathe.

"She told the police you had an argument with your mother and that you intervened when her husband cornered her," he explains. "I paid off the officer in question so the news never made his report. You can relax."

"Can I?" My shoulders slump despite me, my body deflated. "My sister thinks I had something to do with the death of our shitty, deadbeat mother—who, for some reason, Daisy thinks still walks on water."

He tilts his head, unnervingly thoughtful. "I've handled it."

"I don't think you can control the entire world. You *can't*. And you can't control my family. Just like you can't control yours."

"Ah." His gaze sweeps over me. "So now *you* are the criminal mastermind?"

I flinch at the insult. "Maybe I'm just being honest."

"Honest?" he echoes. Only now do I remember that he doesn't like being challenged. He relishes in it. "Your siblings. Do you feel loyalty to them?" Before I can nod in agreement, he adds, "Even if they make your life harder? They weigh you down with their squabbles and indecision. They drain you. Now, say one of them tried to undermine you, ripping away piece by piece everything you sold your soul to gain. What might you do?"

"Slap her," I blurt out. "D-Daisy, I mean. She's... It doesn't matter."

"I see." He nods thoughtfully. "And let's say that *Daisy* owned half of your family's assets, and that by slapping her, you'd be declaring war."

He's talking about more than just my sister. Sevastyn is on his mind again.

Could I declare war on my family?

In a way, I have done just that. Who did Mikie stand by when Daisy and I fought? It wasn't me.

"How would you handle that?" Maxim demands.

I think it over, gazing into my wine. My imagination takes the shade and deepens it into a bloody scarlet. Blood is thicker than water—isn't that how the saying goes?

Or is it *poison* in his case, weighing down your veins and tethering you to a world you might have never chosen for yourself. That's the dangerous part, honestly asking yourself: *if I had to do it all over, would I?*

"I'd try to remember who I am," I say, returning to his dare. "What I've done. Why I've done it. I know that I'm not perfect, but I've never been selfish. I've always been willing to give up everything…"

"And that sacrifice gives you the right to risk upsetting them?" he wonders.

My mouth opens, but I close it and mull the question over. "I deserve to have *something* for me," I finally say. "Even if it won't last. Even if it hurts."

And even if it costs me more than I was ever willing to lose.

"I see." He sits back and drains his own glass. Just as quickly, he pours himself more wine from the bottle. "And if what you want doesn't matter in the grand scheme?"

I think about everything I've done in the name of replacing Melanie. "Does anything really?"

He's quiet for way too long. Nearly a minute. When I finally look up, his expression is unreadable.

"I should start keeping a tally of the times you surprise me."

It's not a compliment, and my heart seizes up in anticipation. Mr. Koslov, terror of the criminal world, doesn't like to be surprised. Least of all by me.

"Tell me something. If you could have one thing in the world, what would it be? Something material," he adds.

"I…" My brain goes blank. "I don't know."

"Don't lie." He palms his wine glass, making the liquid within swish, matching motions of the unreadable emotion flickering in his eyes. "Name it."

"Someplace that's mine, I guess," I stammer. "Where no one could kick me out, or overrun, or rip away."

He processes that in silence, his jaw clenched. Finally, he sits back, placing his hands on the table. "You—" His gaze cuts to something beyond my head and anger distorts his blank expression. "What is it?"

I look back, surprised to find Lucius crossing the deserted dining room. "I tried to stop him, sir," he says, his tone uncharacteristically strained. His eyes cut to a figure entering behind him. "He was persistent."

The entire table jolts as Maxim rises to his feet. "To seek me out…you must have a good reason, Uncle," he says coldly.

The intruder laughs, clapping his hands as he approaches. Sevastyn. His hair is slicked back into a low ponytail, adding a casual contrast to the elegant black suit he wears. Once again, he and Maxim look eerily similar: two halves of the same twisted coin.

"That I do," Sevastyn replies. "But I must say that I didn't expect to find you *here*. And with a toy…" His eyes drift in my direction, inching up my body. Recognition paints them a dangerous shade of black. "So *this* must be the mysterious Francesca." He looks at Maxim, an eyebrow raised. "I didn't realize she was the same—"

"Get out," Maxim growls.

"What, no introductions? I thought you were taught better manners than this, Maxi. Maybe you need another lesson?"

"Do you really believe that you are in the position to order me?"

I jump at the subtle change in Maxim's voice. Gone is the hint of restraint he displayed with me.

He's icier than ever in the blink of a fucking eye. "Now, get out—"

"Be a good boy and send your toy away." Sevastyn dismissively flicks his fingers. "Now."

"No." Maxim slams his hand on the table, knocking his wine glass to the floor. It shatters into a million pieces, and I swear I can see myself reflected in each one, broken just as easily with much less force. "Do not test me."

"I think it's you who forgets your position," Sevastyn replies, dangerously soft. "To refresh your memory, it is a precarious one."

"I will ask you one more time to leave—"

"Oh?" his uncle counters. "So the *boy* thinks he can give ultimatums now? I thought you were too busy fucking your pet while our enemies nip away at your pathetic little enterprise. What? Don't look so surprised, Maxi. I've heard the rumors."

"Rumors?" Maxim echoes. "Or maybe *you've* gotten too bold, Uncle? Sloppy. You're not as careful as you think you've been."

"So challenge me, then," Sevastyn counters, his head cocked. "Or not. Continue to be the little boy who cowers in the corner as he is forced to learn what it really means to be a man—"

"Enough!" Maxim snatches something from the table.

Bam! Air whizzes past my head. In the distance, glass shatters as red liquid explodes against a wall on the other side of the room. Belatedly, my brain makes out the pieces of the wine bottle, raining down like jagged snowflakes.

"I'm not the one who is getting sloppy, Maximov." Sevastyn steps forward, flicking the collar of his jacket, unconcerned by the red liquid staining his white shirt. "The next time you lose your childish little temper, I would encourage you not to miss. Oh, and by the way, consider yourself relieved of the western sector of the city. Anatoli has decided to bestow it upon me instead. Goodnight."

He leaves, chuckling the entire way to the door.

"Get out," Maxim snarls.

I stiffen, still frozen on my chair. That time, the vitriol could have only been directed at me.

I instantly rise to my feet and stagger toward the doorway. Halfway there, my steps change direction. I'm on my knees by the table instead, picking up the shards of his wine glass. I'm not even sure why I'm doing it. Just that I have to. One by one by…

"Enough!" Maxim grabs my wrist, yanking me upright. Fury deepens the black of his irises as he reaches out.

I cringe, covering my face with both hands. I'm braced for a blow, but a heartbeat later, warmth grazes my cheek instead of pain. His finger, I realize as I cautiously let my hands fall.

Meeting his gaze directly is like throwing myself into an inferno, knowing it will burn. Destroy. He peers into my battered shell, staking claim over what shriveled parts of me he hasn't bothered to mark yet—but there's a restraint lurking there. Desperation? Like a diver, clawing his way to the surface, fighting for air. The deep won't drag him down just yet.

It *can't.*

Eventually, his eyelids flutter and the tension drains from him as he yanks me close, grasping my hips. Our foreheads meet and my nostrils flare to breathe him in. Every goddamn inch of rage and muscle and terror. Then, slowly, he pulls away and heads for the door.

With his back to me, his voice lashes out, as sharp as the sting from a whip. "Come."

When we make it back to the suite, he reaches into his pocket and withdraws a cell phone. I suck in a breath as his eyes cut in my direction. For once, he's open.

I can read him like a book, able to decipher every single page. They're all blank, but in a way, it's more telling than paragraphs of text.

In his gaze, I see a warning.

And a plea.

Know your worth, Francesca, he tells me without having to say a fucking word. *Because I've already calculated it.*

"I've made up my mind," he says into the mouthpiece of the phone, turning his attention to the figure on the other end of the call. "We will meet in person to discuss this in full, but..." He looks back at me, his gaze searching mine. "I know where I stand now."

And in a way so do I.

CHAPTER FIFTEEN

I't's funny how being a prisoner warps your entire perception of reality—especially when the bars are in your soul. The first time you wake up, you still feel free. Alive, even. Your sanity may be gone, but you're the one who locked it up and threw away the key.

There's power in that, I guess. Surrender. For the first time in for-fucking-ever, when I peel my eyes open to a darkened room, money isn't the driving force on my brain.

It's panic. It's an instinctive awareness of the man who corrupted me. It's calm. It's fear.

It's *Maxim.*

He's not here. For what feels like hours, I lie still, breathing in his scent, drowning. Eventually I hear the door open but I don't know whether to move or wait. Too many questions linger, demanding to be asked.

Either way, I won't have a real choice in the end.

Huddled beneath the sheets, I listen to his footsteps. Slow. Unsteady.

Unsure?

He circles the foyer like a shark and starts down the hall before changing direction.

An icy dread congeals in my throat. The way he moves is different than the confident prowl I'm used to. Not Maxim.

Lucius, then?

No. My heart pounds as I jump to the next conclusion: an intruder. I dart my gaze to the dresser, but I don't find Maxim's knife. Or even his belt. Desperate for a weapon, I lunge from the bed and grab one of my heels instead.

"I know you're in here," a man calls from down the hall. Something in the raspy, thick accent conjures a terrifying image: Maxim with an older, thinner face and longer hair. "Where is he hiding you, little mouse?" One by one, the foreign footsteps advance in my direction.

Run. The instinct is almost too strong to choke down. Before I can even contemplate hiding, a shadow falls over the doorway and a single thought chases all logic from my brain. *Caught.*

He's tall, the intruder, his face achingly familiar. Sevastyn. "Here you are," he murmurs, leaning against the doorway, his arms crossed. "Maxi's little toy. I have to say…you are beautiful." His eyes flit over what little of my body isn't covered by the sheet. "I'm sure he's told you the opposite. Diminished his attraction to you, even. Maxi always was protective of his trinkets." Standing to his full height, he takes a step closer and I instinctively inch back. "Don't be shy," he scolds, but his smile betrays his enjoyment. "He's kept you busy, I see. I'm surprised he brought you *here*." He glances around the room, his upper lip curled in disgust.

My pulse surges with every second I watch him. "What do you want?"

"Ah… So you are feisty." He chuckles, roving his gaze up to my face. "I knew you were different the moment I saw you, you know. I've only seen him so open with his weakness once before. He's always been a sentimental boy. With toys. With pets."

His tone scratches over my skin, and I draw the sheet tighter around myself. Maxim isn't here. I know that without even looking. Hoping.

"I said, what do you want?"

"Patience." Sevastyn licks his lips and advances a step. He laughs when I flinch and advances another. "You should know exactly why I'm here. My dear nephew deserves nothing less. It's business, my dear. Little Maximov must learn his place." He bares his teeth in a chilling smirk. "I thought making problems for his little enterprise would be enough to get my message across. But it seems he's more… distracted than I thought." He shrugs. "To be honest, I always thought Maxi was much too repressed for a mouthy whore—"

"Get out!"

"Oh, I wish I had time to play with you." He hones his gaze over my throat and I see a hint of the malice he and his nephew share—but it's different in him. Sevastyn lets his darkness consume him, whereas Maxim fights it. "Alas, Maxi must be taught his lesson quickly. I won't violate you," he adds as my nails dig into the fabric of my sheets. "I prefer, let us say, a select breed."

Bile claws up my throat as an image pops into my head, though I'm not sure why. It's how he said that phrase. *Select breed*. Like a little boy with white-blond hair, aching for his mother. Until one horrible day when a monster made him fear showing any ounce of emotion at all.

"I must make my point, however." His hand lashes out so fast that I only catch a flash of shadow before *pain!*

My vision goes black, and when it clears, I only know that I'm on the floor, tasting blood.

"So I apologize if things get…messy. It can't be helped." A heavy hand slams against my lower back, pinning me flat, while another hooks around to capture my throat. Grasping. Squeezing. As if from underwater, I hear Sevastyn murmur, "If you beg, I'll make it quick—"

"No!" Kicking out with my feet is purely instinctual—but my heel connects with bone.

And the man just laughs.

"Oh, you would be so much fun," he murmurs, loosening his grip enough for me to gulp in air. "I can see it now. Why he's kept you like a dog with a bone. Look at me. *Look at me.*" He yanks my face in his direction.

I blink rapidly to clear my vision. Gradually, his face comes into focus.

"Oh yes. There it is." He drags his thumb across my cheek. "That weak hint of desperation. Little Maxim couldn't resist, could he? No." He laughs, shaking his head. "No, I suppose he couldn't. Why? He probably sees himself in you. A desperate, pathetic mutt accustomed to being used by others. Did he ever tell you?" he wonders, lowering his mouth near my ear. "How he became a cripple? I know you've seen them, his injuries... Yes," he decides from my expression alone. "He did. But not all, I suspect. Just the little pieces he can live with. Maximov always was like that. Prone to biding his time like a scheming little mouse. He probably used vague, broad terms to describe it, but shall I tell you the whole truth?"

He shoves me aside and I barely manage to brace my hand against the wall to keep myself from crashing into it.

"His mother was an *artist.*" His nostrils flare as if the word is something filthy found stuck to the bottom of his shoe. "She taught him to paint and sculpt. I think he still does. She used to make him little trinkets. Toys." He chuckles, reliving the memories of Maxim, young and innocent.

"When she died, he kept one—carried it everywhere, despite how it annoyed Anatoli. A little stone cat, I think it was. He called it his '*kotyonok*.' Until one day my father made him smash it using his bare hands. And then..." He looks at me, chuckling, and my stomach churns in grim anticipation. "He had him beaten, but it wasn't enough. Not far enough. Not memorable enough. A boy like that, he needed a different kind of..." A twisted smile shapes his mouth as his tongue traces his bottom lip. "Touch."

No. My mind shies away from what I think a part of me already suspected. I picture the day Maxim brought me to that empty room with the tarp. The pain in his eyes. How lost he looked. Afraid—I can apply that term to him only now.

Not for himself.

But for me.

I will kill you before they do it for me.

"Don't be so surprised," Sevastyn says, still standing above me. "I don't think he even told Anatoli what—"

"You're sick," I croak. "You're a monster."

"I am," he says.

My eyes catch the motion of his shoulder tensing—but it's too late. I can't even brace for the blow. *Wham!* Agony rips through my chest, knocking the air from my lungs. I cough, thrown to my knees, knowing he's behind me.

"What a shame." He crouches and grabs my wrist, rubbing his thumb along my palm. I wrench my arm back and his grip tightens as his gaze latches onto mine. "I'd hate to ruin you too much. You really are a prize. But every good lesson has some cost."

He stands, dragging me with him to the bed. I claw at his grip with my free hand, but he lifts me like I weigh nothing and slams me onto the mattress. Like stone, his weight lands on my chest, pinning me down. Crushing me.

He hits me again, drawing a gasp from my throat.

Nails drawn, I swipe out. Flesh catches beneath my fingertips and I dig as deep as I can, breaking flesh.

Roaring, Sevastyn hits me again—hard. My head lolls as the nerves in my body lose contact with my brain. As my senses return, I find him swiping at his shoulder. His fingers come away red and he frowns, gritting his teeth.

"Feisty little bitch," he snarls, gripping my throat. "He'll throw you away after this, so you know," he gloats as dark spots speckle my vision. Just a few at first. Then an inky coating obscures my sight. "So secretive our Maxi is. In fact, I suspect he'll kill you before you can spill his little secret. But if he doesn't...you can always come to me. I may make an exception..."

He releases my throat, but as I gulp for air, an unfamiliar touch traces my inner thigh. *No!* I buck, clawing at anything I can reach, but he's too heavy. Immovable. *Nonononononono!*

A sharp crack cuts the air before I feel the fire painting my cheek, the result of a slap. Another. My thoughts flood, impossible to decipher.

And all I feel is pain.

CHAPTER SIXTEEN

Hushed voices battle the darkness weighing me down. I'm somewhere enclosed, where everything echoes, way too loud. A room? My eyes won't open. Trying to form a coherent thought is like trying to catch smoke.

I'm floating, but eventually, I can make sense of the words being spoken around me.

"She hemorrhaged," a man says, his voice clinical and unfamiliar. "I doubt there's organ damage, but—"

"When will she wake up?" another man interjects, his tone more strained than I've ever heard it sound. Maxim?

My heart pangs. Something is wrong. Really, really wrong—he's never sounded so cold.

So empty.

"I'm not sure," the first man replies. "All we can do is wait."

"CAN YOU HEAR ME, *KOTYONOK*?" Sensation bleeds through my consciousness for the first time in what feels like an eternity: warm fingers gently parting my hair. "Open your eyes. Look at me."

It's not a request.

I try to obey. But each eyelid weighs a million pounds, impossible to move.

"Francesca." Those creeping fingertips smooth over my forehead and travel down my cheeks. Pain flares in their wake, disrupting my thoughts like a flickering flame. "Look at me."

It's no use. There's no connection between my brain and my mouth. I'm just a conscience tethered to an immovable body. Am I dead?

No. My heart wouldn't be aching if I were.

"Look at me," Maxim commands, but his touch fades away, leaving nothing behind but an empty chill. "Please…"

"SHE'S WAKING UP!"

The high-pitched voice sounds out of place here, insanely loud. Peeling my eyes open takes too much energy. I have to do it in stages, taking in my surroundings via snippets at a time.

"Frankie?"

Something warm lands on my arm. A hand? I blink as a face comes into focus. Small. Round with bright, wide eyes.

"Can you hear me?" Ainsley asks. "Are you okay?"

"Get off of her, Ains!" someone scolds. Mikie. He comes from nowhere and picks up Ainsley by her waist. Then he sets her down in the corner of a spacious room. A hospital room, I think, going off the crisp, clinical smell.

"Where…" My voice is a stranger's rasp. I lick my lips and swallow to strengthen it. "Where am I?"

Mikie glances at someone beyond my line of sight. "The hospital."

"You had an accident," Ainsley says and my stomach sinks. How much do they know?

My memories are a blur, but a few details stick out. *Sevastyn. Pain.*

"That old guy, Lucius, said they were going to sue the other driver," Ray pipes in, coming into view, Ollie in tow. "What a dick—"

"Watch your mouth," Mikie scolds.

"A car accident." I taste the term on my tongue and cringe. So that's the lie he came up with.

"We should let you get some sleep," Mikie says. Like a general, he marshals the others to attention and they stream out one by one. "We'll be back, Frankie. Just get some rest."

My "ACCIDENT" caused contusions over my entire body and left me unconscious for two days. Realizing that puts a million hazy memories into perspective.

The first being Sevastyn. Bits and pieces of that day flicker in and out of my thoughts like a horrifying slideshow. He hit me. Forced me onto the bed…

My brain refuses to show me anything after that.

Deep down, I don't think he raped me. In some ways, his violation was far worse—he marked me. Brutalized me. Toyed with me.

All just to make a point.

And Maxim…

Was he really here or did I just imagine him?

Every minute he stays away, I start to settle on imagined. My only visitors in the next three days are the kids and the odd doctor or nurse. They discuss my care in vague, simplistic tones that give the rouse away. *It's out of my hands. Someone else is pulling the strings and paying the bill.*

Yet he never comes by once. Instead, Lucius appears near the end of the third day, his briefcase in tow.

"Miss Marconi," he says, inclining his head respectively. "Mr. Koslov wanted me to inform you that he is currently out of the country." He pauses as if to let the words sink in one by one. "Any attempts to contact him may go unanswered for a period of time. Meanwhile, if you need anything, I will be able to assist."

He waits as if expecting me to say something. Do something.

When I don't, he inclines his head and leaves. His voice reaches back to me as I finally remember how to move. "Goodnight, Miss Marconi."

A DAY LATER, I'm brought "home" with fanfare. The kids make a show of bringing me lunch in bed and fluffing my pillows.

But the first night passes in dreamlike slow motion.

And the next.

The next.

It's as if the world continues: a boring-ass play, minus one key actor. He disguises his role in my new life, but his interference is painfully clear. Gemma comes to the house to continue my lessons and the bills are magically paid. A mysterious driver appears to chauffer the kids wherever they need to go.

And I'm still a prisoner.

But, as the hours pass, my captor can't even visit my cell once. Days turn into weeks.

My body is a bruised, scabbing mess of flesh, yet...I don't feel a damn thing. I can't feel anything.

"Frankie?"

I look over my shoulder and find Daisy creeping through the doorway.

"You've been in here for hours," she says, glancing around the wide, empty room. "You didn't even eat lunch or dinner—"

"Oh, you're talking to me again?" I snap, only to sigh when she flinches. "I'm sorry. I didn't mean it like that—"

"You've been different," Daisy says. Her eyes well up and she sniffs, swiping at her cheeks with the sleeve of her pink sweatshirt. "It's like you're another person. A zombie. I miss Mama—and I know you hate that," she adds. "But I miss *you* more."

"I'm still me," I rasp, even as I scan my battered limbs without a hint of recognition. "I'm still the same Frankie."

"You're not." Daisy shakes her head, crossing her arms over her chest. She's shaking, sniffling harder as more tears paint her cheeks. "You barely leave the house. You stare into space all the time. Ainsley's afraid of you. She thinks you're dying—"

"I'm still here," I insist. But my voice sounds so fucking weak. I don't know if I'm trying to convince her or myself.

"I miss you," Daisy says. "More than Mama. I miss you—so much. You were always strong, even though you cursed too much and worked too hard. I miss *you*." She lunges, wrapping her arms around my neck, squeezing tight.

She's a little kid again. The one I always had to spend extra time comforting after one of Melanie's fuck-ups. The one so naïve that she never saw the trouble coming.

Or maybe she just pretended not to all this time.

"I'm sorry," I croak into her hair as my stiff limbs cradle her awkwardly. "I'm sorry."

"Just come back," Daisy blubbers. "Come back. Be the old Frankie again. I can't take this anymore."

The old Frankie.

What was her motto? Anything to survive. Even if it meant scraping, and fighting, and stealing.

She would never let herself be thrown away.

She'd fight back.

How?

By beating the master at this own goddamn game.

CHAPTER SEVENTEEN

"You're on fire today!" Gemma exclaims as I hand over a sheet of test questions. She heads to her desk at the front of the classroom and fishes a red pen from a drawer. A few minutes later, she returns the test to me with a score scribbled in the corner: 80%. "You keep this up and you'll have no trouble acing your preliminary finals. Then we can discuss options for majors. Have you thought of any?"

I shake my head. Resurrecting yourself requires baby steps. Waking up. Forcing yourself to breathe. Making yourself focus.

Relying on the relenting passing of time to tide you over, other than a steady pulse of pain. If I focus on that—just moving, and breathing, and living—there isn't room for anything else.

"Well, I think you'll have a great base to build on." She crosses over to her desk. A pinging noise cuts the air, and it must come from her cell phone, because she fishes it from a drawer and eyes the screen. "Oh, my husband is such a nerd," she says, smiling. "It's our anniversary."

Something in her tone cuts through that insistent chorus circling my brain—don't think about him. Anything. *Everything* but him.

"Francesca? Are you all right?"

Crack.

I look up, meeting Gemma's startled gaze, and I can't stop myself from asking, "What was he like with you? Maxim."

Even the sound of his name makes her jump. Her fingers flutter to her throat and she reflexively clutches her cell phone like a child with a teddy bear. Her eyes dart in my direction before lowering to her phone. With a trembling finger, she traces the screen. "Terrifying." She inhales raggedly and looks at me again. "He was terrifying."

She's not lying. Her face is ten shades paler than before and she wobbles to her chair, collapsing onto it. "I was a stupid, desperate kid. I didn't know what to expect. He took one look at me and just...I felt cold." She stares through me, years into the past. "I couldn't go through with it, and he told me to leave. To be honest, I thought he might...I don't know, hurt me or my family. When I received a letter in the mail, I nearly had a heart attack. But it was a check, no strings attached."

For her education—I remember. Maxim Koslov may have trouble keeping the women he claims to crave, but he has no problem being strictly transactional.

"Are you okay?" Gemma stands and approaches me, placing her hand on my shoulder. "Is he…Is he hurting you?" She glances around the room, still clutching her neck. "Maybe we can—"

"I'm fine," I say, rising to my feet. Her concern feels far too real. Earnest. Her wide eyes hone in on my bruises and I know the conclusions she jumps to. Abuse. Violence. From him.

Any sane person would think the same damn thing.

Maybe they'd have a point—though the only true damage Maxim Koslov has inflicted on me is on my psyche. My fucking soul.

"Frankie?" Gemma brushes her hand along my shoulder. "Are you sure you're okay?"

"Y-yes." Swallowing hard, I force myself to smile. "I really am fine. Thanks for everything."

I leave her staring after me in a daze, but I don't have any room left in my head to care. He warned me: I'm not worth fighting for. Dying for.

But fuck it.

He can tell me as much to my face.

CHAPTER EIGHTEEN

The first place I go to turns me away. I look too young, they say.

Too young. I almost laugh until I catch sight of myself in a reflection on a glass window on my way out. A wide-eyed stranger stares back. Shit. It's like my time with Maxim has aged me backward, stripping away the battle scars I've built up over the years. I've lost that spark in my eye. That gleam that made any man I walked past do a double take and clutch his wallet. That hard-as-fuck, tough-as-nails glimmer that warned bitches like Melanie to back the fuck off.

I've lost myself.

Now, I just look pathetic. A little girl lost, caught in the wake of a monster who dishes out the only candy worth having. *Pain.* She's grown addicted to his bitter sugar and can't stop licking her lips for more.

But, already, I'm remembering what it feels like to go without it.

It feels like desperation.

The second place I go to doesn't turn me away.

"You start tonight," the owner tells me as he leans against a barstool and flicks a disapproving glance at my plain, white dress. "Make sure you fucking change first. We don't do the kiddie shit here. Thongs and lace."

He slaps my ass on my way out, and it's only now that it sinks in. This is *real*. I'm in the real world again, and the pain here doesn't feel so good. My ass smarts. My throat tightens.

But no one steps from the shadows to avenge the assault and I just keep walking.

I waste the day lurking in another bar until the hour of my first shift. When I return to the club, I'm directed to an older blond woman who glances me over and sighs.

"This way."

She turns on her heel and cuts a path through a barroom packed with sweaty motherfuckers clutching loose dollar bills and jostling for better seats around the stage. They whoop and holler while a woman wearing a bad wig strips her skimpy lingerie and shakes her ass to the tune of a rap song blaring through unseen speakers.

It's nothing like the dangerous displays of flesh Maxim puts on in his club.

Not that it fucking matters.

I cut my teeth on places like this. You've been to one strip club, you've been to them all. Unless it happens to be owned by a psychopathic Russian…

Snap out of it. I shake my head to clear it as I follow the woman into a narrow room lined with mirrors and clothing racks.

"Pick something," she tells me, nodding her chin toward a rather paltry selection of silk and lace.

None of it is hand-tailored or of the finest quality. It's cheap, bargain bin stuff, probably from JC Penney. When I finger a black bralette, it chafes.

"You sure you're up to this, sweetheart?" the woman asks, frowning as she looks me over for the second time.

The mirror in front of me reveals just what she sees: a skinny bitch with wild hair and haunted eyes. Her face is bruised, and cuts litter her body like the glitter my tour guide has sparkling on her skin.

She's pathetic.

She's not *me*.

But when I speak, her lips move. "I'm fine."

"Whatever you say," the woman says warily.

To prove her wrong, I strip my dress and start to pull on a set of black lingerie.

Rather than look impressed, she winces. "Oh, honey!"

Her gaze is on my upper thigh. Mainly the name carved into my skin.

"Your man doesn't play around, does he?"

He doesn't.

But he isn't mine, either.

I know without having to search the corners of the barroom that he's not here lurking when I take my place on stage. As the lights dim, I'm left alone in a puddle of dingy, artificial glow, unguarded by my master, who doesn't seem interested in claiming me anymore.

Instinct guides my movements as I gyrate in a circle to some sleazy pop song. They claim they don't want "kiddie shit" here, but that's what I feel like: a kid sticking her fingers into electrical sockets, waiting for the moment I'll be scolded…

Only that moment doesn't come as jeers and taunts rise from the crowd, demanding I strip. "Take it off!"

My fingers shake as they creep up my rib cage. I finger the edge of my lacy bra once. Twice. The tease earns a round of groans, but I'm not playing the same game they seem to be.

I'm more attuned to my body than I've ever been. I wait for the telltale hitch in my throat. That uncanny ice-running-down-my-spine sensation that warns me I'm being watched. The cold, chilling realization that a predator is nearby with me in his sights.

I'm breaking his fucking rules for everyone to see.

But I'm never punished for the transgression.

I strip the bra to applause and cheers. The money flying in my direction is only a fraction of what Maxim could offer.

Maybe I'm stupid for spitting on that.

Or maybe…

I'm just fucking insane.

I DON'T GO HOME. I don't even call the kids to let them know where I am. Instead, I use what little money I earned my first night to rent a motel room, the cheapest I can. The walls are as thin as tissue paper, the door even thinner. But they hold the entire time I toss and turn on the crappy bed.

Alone, I return to the club and dance the next night, scraping my meager wages together.

I do the same the next night.

And the next.

Four nights in and only now does it sink in. Reality. This new, cold world I've found myself in, where I'm numb to the drooling looks of horny men. Only on this night does someone touch me, hooking their fingers into my thong when I stray too close to the edge of the stage.

Asshole. My thoughts short-circuit as I wait for the disgust I should feel. The instinctive need to scurry away or fight.

Instead, I feel…

Fire? It sears through my veins as a warning. The first real fucking thing I've felt in so long. Greedily, my fingers fly out, desperate to chase it. Extend it. I find a meaty, groping hand that clenches mine in shock and nearly drags me off the stage and onto some asshole's lap.

He chuckles, clenching my ass so tightly that I gasp. He smells like beer and sweat, and my heart races, pounding out a frantic melody.

Air sticks to the inside of my lungs. God, it's like I'm waking up. I feel everything. Sharp, ragged fingernails scraping my flesh. Harsh, unsteady breathing on my neck. The sweet, terrible clench of foreboding in my belly that warns me of danger like nothing else.

Alarm bells go off in my mind. *Mayday! Mayday!*

I'm shaking before I spot him in the corner of the room. He's dressed casually tonight, a realization that makes my throat tighten. A black shirt is lazily buttoned to reveal a sliver of the muscled chest underneath. Flashing eyes meet mine and the full breadth of my fear slams into me like a freight train. Have I gone insane?

Maybe.

He leans against the wall, his head tilted appraisingly. The pad of his thumb strokes his chin in a spine-curling rhythm. Slow. Steady. He watches me the same way he observes those beaten, broken chunks of marble left over from his sculpting sessions. Which is the fastest way to sweep the mess up and toss it aside?

Most nights, he just leaves it there for a maid to clean, I assume.

But now?

His jaw isn't clenched in the way I've come to expect. His shoulders are relaxed, free of tension. The only ominous clue I have to latch onto are his eyes. They smolder in the glow of the stage lights, fixated on my position without revealing a shred of what he's thinking.

But I just *know*.

My eyelids flutter at the feeling. It's raw, like I sliced myself open on a jagged piece of glass. A million things rush to pour from the wound all at once. Vital things. Pain. Fear. *Sanity.*

But at least I'm fucking feeling something. Tears prickle behind my eyes as my head swims beneath the aching burn of emotion.

"You gonna move or what, baby?" the asshole whose lap I'm on asks.

I move, all right. Arching my hips back and forth doesn't earn a single reaction from the only client who matters. He could be watching paint dry as far as anyone else is concerned.

But with every slow, deliberate motion, my heart threatens to beat its way from my chest. Save itself. Flee. An overwhelming sense of danger descends like a cloud, looming above me. *Doom. Doom.* It's like someone is here, whispering the word into my ear the longer I grind on the sleazy stranger.

The longer I extend my disobedience.

The perv hisses in anger when I finally climb off him and blindly stagger to the stage.

But it's too little too late. The music trails off, followed by one terrifying sound that cuts through the murmurs of the crowd and the hammering thud of my pulse.

Thwack.

Thwack.

Clapping? The racket is made by just one man, who's leaning against his chosen corner. The slow, deliberate crack of his palms meeting matches the way my heart thunders and slows. His eyes hone in on my own, *seeing* me.

Punishing me.

Stripping me bare with a soul-crushing promise.

I've broken our "arrangement."

And the feral gleam in his eyes reveals that he's more than willing to devise a fitting punishment.

CHAPTER NINETEEN

He pulls away from the wall with the agility of a wolf. Heedless of anyone watching, he mounts the stage, swallowing the distance between us with slow, deliberate strides. He comes close. So fucking close... My nostrils flare to capture his scent. *Ice, winter, danger.* Cotton grazes my bare skin, sparking the urge to fight or flee. Before either instinct can win, time runs out.

He leans in for the kill and I'm paralyzed as warm lips brush my cheek and raise goosebumps in their quest for my ear. He inhales, tasting my sweat mingled with the stench of a stranger.

And I tense as I wait for retribution.

"That...that was a beautiful show," he murmurs instead, his tone level with each word. Flat.

There's something I didn't notice before in his hand. As he draws back, he lets it fall to the floor at my feet without explanation.

My gaze lowers, seeking it out as my fingers quiver. He brought me a rose. Its petals dot the floor as he leaves, taking the fire with him.

The damn thing consumes my attention, even as someone tries to motion me off the stage. Material is wrapped around it, mangling the lower petals. It's a tiny strip of paper, tied with a scarlet ribbon. An address is printed on it, along with a simple message.

Wear the dress.

I stagger backstage and find a strip of silk waiting for me, draped over one of the vanities. Another folded note rests beside it, graced with crisp handwriting. *Refuse me now and I'll end this.* My heart skips as I read those words a second time. Again.

End this. I should crave that outcome. An end to this pain. This tumultuous hell. No more feeling him in every pore.

The promise haunts me as I scan the page and notice all the little details I didn't before. His hand shook as he wrote this. He pressed down hard too. Hard enough to slice the paper beneath the strokes of my name. *Francesca.* It's scribbled there at the bottom, and each inked letter glows, a searing reminder of the brand on my thigh.

The dress itself is beautiful. Too beautiful. A plunging neckline shows off what the dominant male I know wouldn't, giving a greedy glimpse of my cleavage. Too much. However, apart from the daring cut, it's shapeless.

Just thin silk rasping over battered flesh. A sudden realization makes my chest tighten.

It's made for ripping. For tearing.

I might as well be wearing nothing at all.

I'm tempted to take it off. Walk away. He's given me so many chances before. Maybe this is the one out I'm finally willing to take? Or not... I swallow hard as my fingers graze the material gathered at my hip. I flick it once. Twice. With each touch, I wrestle with the obvious question.

To stay or go?

Unsure, I turn and observe myself in the mirror. My mouth curls into a snarl of disgust. Fuck. Maxim's pet is a creature I hate. She looks nothing like me. The girl staring back is too thin. Too fragile. Too broken. Her brown eyes are dilated and desperate. *Hungry.*

And not for food.

Not for money.

I turn my back on her and leave the club, pushing through anyone who stands in my way. It's only when I'm outside that I start to wonder just what I'll do. Run? The thought doesn't even finish forming before a black car pulls up alongside the curb, cutting my escape off.

Maxim isn't the one driving, and the stranger says nothing as I hesitate. Slowly, I reach for the handle. Pull back. Eventually, I climb in, and he takes off the moment I'm seated, pitching me headlong into another dizzying nightmare.

This one begins the same way our first official meeting did. I'm brought to a restaurant in the richer part of town, where the price for valet is more than a month's rent.

Goosebumps prickle my skin as I eye the grand exterior. Sleek glass gives a breathtaking glimpse within. Dark walls. Dim lighting. The perfect lair for a beast who craves discretion.

I know how this part of the story will unfold. I'll wander down this new rabbit hole and find my monster waiting for me within. He'll give me a new ultimatum. Only this time...

This time, I'll refuse. Walk away.

I won't crawl into Wonderland again.

Where did this newfound resolve come from? I don't know. It races through my veins like smoke, nearly impossible to catch and identify. God, I try. I want to cling to it. But the moment my eyes focus on the figure approaching my side of the car, that frail emotion dies.

Someone scribbled into the margins of this chapter, adding in things that shouldn't exist. Like Maxim, opening my door and offering a hand to help me out. He shouldn't be here. Not like this. Waiting for me. Claiming me with no time for me to compose my thoughts.

"Francesca."

I shudder at the grated cadence to my name. He grinds it between his teeth, the only clue as to the emotions smoldering beneath the icy exterior. His face reveals nothing. Dressed to kill in black, he could almost pass for a normal man.

Almost.

But those eyes belong solely to a predator fixated on my bared skin and fluttering pulse. I stare at his palm without reaching for it. The smooth skin disguises so much potential for violence. The fingers quiver ever so slightly, echoing the unsteady energy running through my entire body. I'm a live wire. He's a fucking lightning storm, threatening to overload my fragile senses.

Obliterate me.

A breath I didn't even realize I was holding escapes in a rush as he stands back, returning his hand to his side. A quick jerk of his chin, however, conveys the command he doesn't issue out loud. One I don't dare disobey. *Come.*

I scramble out onto the curb. After two frantic steps on my own, I think he'll let me walk unaccosted. Yeah, right. The heavy hand settling against my lower back shatters that delusion. His heat radiates into my skin. Figuratively. Literally. I'm breathing in flames, exhaling smoke, smoldering from the inside out like the electrical fire that destroyed our house a few years back. None of us smelled the stench of burning until it was too late.

"You're back." I don't know how I manage to question him considering that my lungs are devoid of air.

His palm flexes, guiding me toward the restaurant's entrance. From the corner of my eye, I see his jaw clench for a second and then loosen, which betrays effort on his part to stay in control.

"For how long?" I ask, goading him.

He doesn't give me an answer as he leads me inside what appears to be a private dining room, away from the front-facing windows. Burgundy wallpaper decorated in golden designs forms a beautiful prison. There's only one table here. Two chairs. *One* dinner guest, who's standing beside me. His hand presses impatiently against my flesh, withdrawing only when I'm close enough to a chair to sit.

But I don't. Not even when he takes the seat opposite me and rests his hands over a pristine, white tablecloth. At a glance, a naïve woman might mistake his expression for one of calm.

But those hands betray him. They flex against the table's surface, the knuckles whitening with every second I stay standing.

"Sit, Francesca." He nods to the chair before me.

I don't move. "I'm…" I trail off, unable to put into words just what I mean to say. In the end, I blurt out the argument circling my brain in a morbid loop. "You left. I thought you were done with me—"

"You are making this…difficult."

My throat hitches at the unmistakable strain in his voice—the first slip in his façade. "Good," I say hoarsely. "Because it's been *hell* for me." I flinch at the vitriol tainting my own voice. Fuck it. "Tell me why I shouldn't leave—"

"I know you're upset." His eyes only reflect more tightly controlled restraint. "Sit."

I bite my lower lip. It's not quite the dangerous octave I've come to fear, but it's close to it. In the end, I perch myself at the end of the chair and brace my hands on my thighs.

"We will talk, and this time, no one will interrupt us," Maxim says, speaking each word deliberately. Almost as if he's hammering them out between his teeth, sculpting the illusion of calm the way he does marble. "How do you feel?"

I blink. On cue, I should spit out my tired line. *Fine.* "Someone hurt me," I croak instead. "And you weren't there."

He flinches, punched. Just as quickly, he cocks his head and his eyes flash. "No. I wasn't."

"And now? What?" My eyes water, overflowing within seconds. "I'm supposed to just…sit in a cage like a good little pet, while you—"

"I needed time to think," he says over me. "Time to reassess my priorities."

"Priorities," I parrot. "Maybe I've reassessed my priorities, too? I think I need a new client—"

"I made a mistake in thinking you'd be patient," he says before I can finish. "I should have known better than to underestimate you. Again." As he speaks, his hand drifts toward a polished set of silverware spread out in front of him. His thumb dances a slow path from the tines of a fork to the edge of a silver butter knife as if deciding between the two. A tool or a weapon? "But you're not angry that I caught you." He nods, seemingly to himself. "No... You enjoy this. You enjoy pushing me to the fucking brink."

"Stop!" I cringe and push back from the table, ignoring the telltale clenching of his jaw. "You're insane."

"And *you* live for it," he counters, still seated, still eerily calm. His thumb continues to stroke the edge of the knife. Faster. Harder, leaving streaks of sweat along the metal. "I saw the truth tonight. That look in your eye. You're wet already, thinking of the things I will do to you."

He's lying. My body feels heavy because I'm afraid. So afraid that I'm aching. Burning. Dying from anticipation.

"And the things I *will* do to you," he muses, his voice thickening. "Whatever punishment you think you've earned, I can assure you that you won't come close."

My mind skips ahead, conjuring a million horrific tortures. Whips. Chains. Pain.

"Then," he says as if factoring in every single fantasy, "we will be, as they say, *even*."

Even? Something he said weeks ago sticks in my brain. *If I hurt you again, you have my permission…*

"Like you have the right—" My breathing hitches and a guttural sound cuts into my thoughts, setting every nerve in my body on edge. It came from him, ripped right from his chest. A growl.

"I can smell you from here," he warns, his throat jerking around a harsh swallow. His eyes flash and train on my throat, tracing every nervous swallow I take. "You deserve to be ripped raw for what you've done. Bitten until you know you're mine. Fucked senseless for every man who's seen you. One hundred and fifty-seven. I've been keeping count."

He says it all without a damn given for any waiter or waitress who might overhear. But we're alone by design, I realize after a quick glance around.

This display of domination is solely for me.

"You *want* me to," he declares coarsely. His knuckles whiten further as his fingers flex, bunching the tablecloth with every tense motion. "So ask for it."

"Why? So you can leave the country the second you feel like it?" My knees are shaking, knocking against one another. My thighs are clenched together so tightly that sweat drips between them. God, I hope it's sweat. "I thought you were done—"

He laughs and the rich sound startles me into silence. "You know, any other pet would take that as a mercy," he says. "A sane woman. They'd be relieved."

His tone is too hard. It's not a joke.

"But not *you*," he continues, his lips parting into a dangerous shadow of a smile. He's never looked more terrifying than he does now: painfully, insanely honest. "You don't want to share your pain. So fucking greedy, you are. You want my sole attention, *kotyonok*. You want to be the only little doll I get to fuck."

My cheeks flame. "But you don't want to keep me."

"*Oh*?"

I've barely processed the motion of standing when his hand strikes the table so hard that his knife goes flying and slides across the wooden floor. His sharp intake of breath is my only warning before I feel him. His hand cinches around my wrist, imparting a strength that makes me gasp. Groan.

A monstrous crash shakes the room to its core. The table being shoved aside? No, a giant, barreling toward me.

Pain. Nails sink into my flesh as he grabs me by the shoulder and yanks me back, lifting my feet from the floor. I kick out, but it's no use. He spins me around and crushes me to the wall. His chest feels hard against my back, his teeth catching my earlobe and biting down. It's merely a taste of his anger, and the brief, sharp pain has me writhing against burgundy wallpaper.

But it's not enough. Never enough.

"I will give you what you want," he swears. "But first, you admit it. Tell me, little *kotyonok*. Tell me what you need."

My brain shies away from the question, chanting an answer that's become a mantra. *Nothing. Nothing. Just money. Nothing else.* But the lie doesn't leave my throat, and I go limp, sandwiched between him and the wall. What do I need?

I scrape my nails against the harsh surface beneath me, seeking the delicious burn. Any pain I can find on my own. Clarity. I crave it. Whatever I feel is only a faint echo of what the creature behind me promises. His breath alone is a tempting burn against my flesh.

Too. Fucking. Real.

"Say it," he coaxes, destruction promised in every grated syllable. Thick fingers fist through my hair and tighten, making tears burn behind my eyes. He tugs his fist. "Tell me—"

I groan, smearing drool along the design of a gilded fern. "You tell me," I choke out.

He pulls on my hair so hard that I'm forced to arch my back and focus my blurred vision on the ceiling. A scream escapes my throat, but it's in vain. No one's coming. Not a waitress or another diner.

I'm alone in hell with him.

And this time, he won't let me escape.

My heart hammers at the chilling realization. My lips moisten. Throat swallows. Legs tighten...

"Fuck, even the thought of it arouses you," Maxim accuses. He barely sounds human anymore. Just a pained creature who communicates in growls and grunts. Primal. Ruthless. Animal.

He's unashamedly harsh, grinding his erection against my ass, teasing me with the brutal fullness. Moist heat floods my inner thighs, readying for the violence promised. If I let him, he'll break me. Ruin me.

A thought races across my mind before I can smother it: *I want him to.*

"I'll tell you what I want. I promise I'll..." His teeth seize the skin along my collar and bite down to the point where it stings. But not enough to bleed. Not enough to really hurt. Not enough to make me feel how only he can.

Sharp.

Clear.

Alive...

"I'll say it first. Is that what you fucking want? I want *you*," he admits, his voice a nearly unintelligible octave. "You... begging me to stop. Knowing I won't. I want you raw. Wet. Fucking. Screaming. Fuck, I crave *you*—"

He stops making sense and just mutters nonsense. Violent things. Brutal things. Tempting, fucking, twisted, insane goddamn things.

"But you..." Ragged breaths slice my words into gnarled bits. "Let me go. Again. You're always letting me go! Do you want to know what he said? Sevastyn?" I twist, spitting the words in his face. "He said you wouldn't want me after. And he was fucking right!"

"No." Without warning, he wrenches the sleeve of my dress down one arm, baring my breast to the mercy of his fingers. Heat. Tearing. Ice. He cups me in his palm, capturing my heart through layers of flesh and bone.

Groaning, he squeezes.

"Never. You are mine." He finds my nipple between the pads of two fingers and crushes it.

My moan drips from me in heaving, disjointed cries. They nearly drown out what he says next. What he breathes into me. What madness he confesses.

"I will *always* crave this tight fucking cunt. This greedy little whore who screams my name when she comes for me. On me. I want to own her. One day...I will destroy her. I'll rip her into fucking pieces—"

"Stop lying."

"Enough!" he roars deafeningly. It's a sound I've never heard him make. His hands grip me tighter than ever. Bruising. Breaking. "Do you know where I went? I needed to think. Are you worth it? My money, my world, all of it—"

"Stop!" I go limp, choking on tears. "I get it. I'm fucking not. I get it! I'm fucking worthless."

He draws back too suddenly. I have to cling to the wall for balance and wind up sinking to my knees. My throat aches, but that voice didn't come from me. No. Not that pathetic fucking plea. I haven't heard that girl in so damn long. Not since she uttered the same words to a shitty-ass mother who never cared.

No one ever cared.

But he listens, feasting on every whispered word and sob.

I'm cutting myself open on the remnants of his soul.

And. It. Hurts.

Like nothing else.

"But I don't care if you think that. I...I'm tired. I'm done." I try smothering the words into my hands, but he's there, crouching behind me to tear them away. "I'd rather walk away for good than constantly have you rip me *open*."

"When I learned what he did, I realized something." His palm captures my throat, tightening. "Nothing is more important than family."

"Stop." I pant. My cheeks are wet, my chest aching. But there's no use fighting him now. Squeezing my eyes shut, I surrender. "I...I can't—"

"But *they* are not my family." His voice resonates in my bones, unbearably deep.

The only way to block him out is to cover my ears like a fucking child. "Please stop."

"I don't have the right to, but I'm asking. Give me one more night. One more day. If you can do that, you know where to find me."

He steps back and I watch him through blurred vision.

"Wait—"

"I need you to come to me one last time," he says. "One last chance for you to decide…"

Decide what exactly?

He leaves without saying.

And I'm too fucking tired to guess.

CHAPTER TWENTY

As the hours pass, I can't ignore this little voice in my head telling me that I am losing the bet already. He said that, when I'm ready, I would know where to find him, but with a man like him, there is only one domain where he would cement a deal like this: the closest equivalent he has to hell.

I'm shaking as I finally drag myself from my motel room, dressed in a shirt and a pair of jeans, and find a car waiting for me out front. One word and the driver knows the way. Twenty minutes later, he brings me right up to the mouth of the club and that shimmering entrance.

There's no one waiting for me out front. I have to enter alone, pushing the main door open before wandering through that cold, foreboding archway. The intensity of the club hits me all at once: murmured voices, low music, sex crackling in the air.

My eyes are automatically drawn to the stage, just in time to witness the climax of the current show. A buxom redhead is lying across a dais while a man wielding a whip flogs the hell out of her ass from behind. She's pretty, making enough noise to sell the performance.

But it's her costar who commands the stage and steals the limelight.

He's bathed in the scarlet glow of the club, and I've never seen anyone look so menacing. So fucking powerful: a creature of sin and perfection with a devilish temper to show for it. His hair streams back from his face like a mane, his expression feral as he gives the redhead another brutal taste of the whip.

She throws her head back sensually, howling in pain.

The crowd fucking drools.

But then the show abruptly comes to a halt. Every bit as revealing as a spotlight, two black eyes hunt me down where I'm standing. His hand falls, the whip striking nothing but air as a frown twists his mouth. There is no ounce of shame in his expression: just a dare I'm not brave enough to answer.

Why are you here, kotyonok?

I don't know what draws me forward, forcing me to sidestep a well-dressed couple intent on creating their own show. The closer I come to the stage, the more impressed I am by the setup, despite myself. Three black steps built into the side of the structure allow someone to mount it seamlessly from the audience.

The moment the sole of my sneaker strikes the first step, a shadow falls over me and I find a monster impatient to dish out my punishment. He doesn't say a fucking word. His eyes merely track my ascent as I mount the second step and cling to the wall for balance. Somewhere within the past few minutes, the redhead disappeared. The dais is empty: a slab of black marble beckoning me closer.

Beyond the stage, the entirety of the club stretches out, and every patron watches with avid interest as a heavy hand cups the back of my throat and herds me forward. I'm blinded by the blood-red glow of the lights as Maxim trails a thumb over the corner of my mouth.

When he nudges me forward, I comply, resting my upper body over the cold slab of marble, both hands braced on either side of me. The moment I'm prone before him, hungry fingers wrench up the back of my shirt and tug on my jeans, baring my ass. A weighted second passes, as if he's giving me the chance to resist. Run. I don't, and not even a second later, something whistles through the air—it's like he can't control the whip fast enough.

The first blow isn't a love tap. The leather bites deep, leaving a stinging pinch I feel all the way in my goddamn core. The answering cry rips out of me, too raw to be held back.

Not that I even try to.

The next blow jolts me forward onto the tips of my toes, forcing my fingers to scramble for purchase over the marble. I'm bleeding: a searing welt too shallow to drip. The blood ekes out slowly instead, smearing my skin, tainting the air like perfume. Another hit draws a real cry out of me, one that echoes above every other sound.

And for the first time in so long, I can think. I can feel.

Everything.

Pain returns like an old friend, assaulting me at the urging of a sadistic master—and he makes damn sure I suffer for every second he had to wait for me.

It feels like an eternity—and every stinging blow only feeds the fire surging through my skin. Consuming me. My cheek is pressed flat against the marble when I finally sense him staggering closer, his hips brushing the back of my ass. Unrelentingly hard, his erection pulses against the fabric of his pants, hungry for my skin. For me.

Another sound tears out of me before I can choke it down. Wet heat clamps over my earlobe as I writhe against his hardness.

"Did you think it would be this easy?" a demon growls into my ear, yanking on my hair when I don't answer. He maintains his hold, even as I stagger to regain my balance—but it's a damn good thing he does.

I've never felt this unsteady before; it's like I'm drunk, intoxicated by his scent. The rest of the club is a smear of blurred features and meaningless faces. My sole focus is on the creature behind me.

With little care for my modesty, he wrenches my jeans down my legs. Panties next. My shirt, he rips from my collar down, baring my breasts and leaving me naked. In front of everyone. One firm yank on my shoulder twists me around to face him. His eyes probe my own as he steers me back, forcing me to climb back onto the stone slab, his body between my legs.

I get the briefest taste of his erection brushing my inner thigh before he kneels. *Oh god.*

His palm flattens against my stomach, pinning me down and throwing my upper body across the marble altar. My head dangles off the edge and all I see are scarlet and shadow before I feel the splash of his breath on me— followed by his tongue. His *teeth*.

My eyes roll to the back of my goddamn head as the noise from the crowd swells with murmurs of interest. This isn't the typical act they're used to. With ruthless, brutal determination, Maxim Koslov shreds the script.

Right here, on his knees, in front of what feels like the whole damn world, he fucks me with his tongue. Eats me out. Devours me.

There's no preamble like last time. No point to prove.

Two of his fingers spread me open while his tongue strikes deep, and my entire body jerks as it registers the invasion: thick, hot, burning…too much…*god.*

I buck my hips, chasing the sensation, and the nails of his right hand dig into my ass in retaliation. The burning sting has barely coursed through me before he changes his tactic and aims higher, going for the jugular. Pain and pleasure are my only clues to illustrate what he's doing to cause that harsh, aching sensation in my core: grinding my clit between his teeth.

And then my brain ceases any coherent thought altogether. I stop tracking his movements and I just fucking feel...

Everything.

In the end, he doesn't let me come; he drags me to the edge. Right when my toes curl. When my chest heaves, my nipples stabbing at nothing. Right when I can't think or *do* anything else but explode...

That's when he pulls back, his lips glistening, his eyes on fire. One of his hands shoots into the air as if beckoning someone closer.

Or something from the ceiling...

I catch the glint of silver from the corner of my eye before I witness the object being lowered on a rope as if on cue. It's a hook, the end pointed toward me. With one hand, Maxim grabs it while the other manipulates the whip. He turns his wrist clockwise, winding the leather strap around his knuckles.

Somehow, I know to lift my arms, raising them high above my head. A shiver runs through me at the harsh contrast of his heat and the cold leather as he wraps the loose end of the whip around my wrists, binding them tightly. I have no choice but to scoot forward to the edge of the slab as he lifts my bound wrists so that the hook catches the center bit of leather between them. Then he steps back and the pressure in my arms grows taut. I have to strain on the tips of my toes—until even that isn't enough. Within a matter of seconds, I'm suspended by my hands, dangling completely at his mercy.

Higher and higher, my body is hiked by the hook, until I have to stare down to meet Maxim's gaze. His narrowed eyes trace my captive form, honing in on my heaving chest, my breasts swaying for his attention.

I try to close my eyes. Block out the tension swirling through my veins, growing hotter with every step I hear him take—but he is a ruthless master. Callused fingers grab my hip, holding me steady as his body edges in closer. Too close. The ragged vibration of every inhale he takes electrocutes me. My skin is paper, his touch a ravenous fire threatening to burn me alive.

And the worst part?

My inner thighs are already slick, craving the destruction.

"Look," Maxim commands into my ear. With one hand, he manipulates my body just enough for me to see the shape of the crowd lurking behind us. "They're watching you. They smell you." He inhales too, the sound reverberating down my spine. "How you weep for me. *Fuck,* I can taste you."

The raw lust in his voice steals my breath away. I've never been this terrified. This damn *alive*, on the edge of pain and insanity. Too many men have had my body to even count, but none have made me crave them back. Like heroin. Like air. Deep inside, muscles I didn't even know I had clench and unclench, desperate for something to cling to.

"Look at me."

His gaze is feral when I do: all teeth and those eyes crazed with hunger. I nearly choke on the cry that threatens to break free as he muscles his way between my legs, jarring my precarious balance. The rasp of his pants against my inner thighs clashes with the throbbing pain building in my shoulders. It's too fucking much.

"I will not play with you tonight," Maxim tells me, his voice gritted. "There is a reason why you came back to me. Can you tell me?" A cruel thumb nudges my chin, forcing me to meet his gaze again, our frantic breaths mingling. "Hmmm?"

My body jolts. I *know*. Every cut in my flesh stings in a mocking symphony. Away from him, none of it feels strong enough. *I'm* not strong enough...

And, damn it, I don't want to be anymore.

"Say it," he goads, nipping my throat, a taste of what I crave. "Your safe word," he adds when my brain stalls, unsure of what he means. "Say it now."

If it was hard to say it before, it should feel impossible to now. My leverage. My sanity... All of it is tied to two little words that spill from my tongue on command. "I'm...happy."

His unstable chuckle swallows up the words and it's like I never said them at all. "Now, beg me to fuck you. And know that, the moment I enter your cunt this time, there will be no more lies. No more games."

No more safety net, a part of me cries, filling in the blanks of what he doesn't say.

"You can still run." Another dizzying kiss lands on my shoulder, giving way to raking, biting teeth. "Maybe I'll even let you go. But we both know..." His hand slips between my legs, batting the dangling limbs apart and gliding along the outside of my pussy. One thrust of his thumb and I'm jerking on the hook, swaying back and forth, a scream trapped in my throat. "We both know the truth, don't we, *Francesca*?"

Hearing my name come out of his mouth, thick with need? It shatters me. Suddenly, even the brush of his fingertips stings like the touch of a live wire. I can't breathe. Can't think. I'm so damn close...

"I will only tell you this once." His tongue blazes a trail along my jaw, inching toward my mouth. Once he reaches his destination, his lips settle over mine, allowing me to feel every uttered word. "Tell me why you're here."

"Because... Because I'm yours."

One minute, he's holding me steady in the air. The next, he's ramming into me, with one brutal hand on my ass while the other sinks into my hair, forcing my mouth against his.

We don't fuck.

We come un-fucking-done.

I scream.

He growls, pistoning his hips until the friction sets me on fire. I'm eaten alive by the flames, watched by countless people, consumed by the only man who matters.

"This"—he thrusts, stretching me wide while his free hand assaults my throbbing clit—"is"—another thrust—"pain. I feel it…" Awe chokes his voice as he thrusts again and the motion triggers his release, which draws out a roar he bellows into my skin. "*What have you done to me?*"

I'm on cloud fucking ten, but I still know I'll always remember those words. How he said them: raw, without a damn for who could hear.

"What will I do to you?" he rasps next, sounding crazed. Mindless. One last pump of his hips grinds the rest of his release into my ravaged pussy and I go under. Maybe I only imagine the words I hear next. "You are mine."

He lets his ownership hang in the air, which is every bit as powerful as the orgasm ripping me to pieces.

CHAPTER TWENTY-ONE

S urvival is something you can't ever regret—I know that better than anyone.

Whatever it takes. No matter the cost. You lie, cheat, and steal if you have to. Your actual feelings never matter.

Until they *do* and it's all you can do to just lie there in a daze, hemorrhaging something more vital than blood.

I've never felt this kind of pain before. It's consuming, biting deeper than anything physical. It's in my soul: a wound left gaping open and I don't know how to staunch the flow. Something tells me that Band-Aids won't work in this scenario.

Maybe it's pride I'm losing—the one thing I always told myself I still had. Not even hooking deprived me of it. Neither did Melanie or any of the shit she put me through. I was still Francesca Marconi through it all, one tough-ass bitch.

But without even trying, Maxim Koslov made me surrender the only thing of value I had left. The worst part?

I gave it to him willingly.

Ain't that one for irony.

My exhausted psyche can't admit defeat just yet and clings to any other alternative. This is just a nightmare... It isn't real. As if to prove me wrong, reality returns in full force. It's cold here. I'm numb. It's loud, a million sounds battling for supremacy. Murmurs. Music. My head spins, struggling to piece it all together from the chaos of my memory. *The club. The stage. Maxim.*

Too late.

Ruthless fingers rake through my hair, electrocuting the nerves along my scalp. My shoulders are on fucking fire—I feel that first and nearly choke on a gasp as my eyes fly open to a hazy blur of red and black. I have to blink a few times before I can make out anything of substance, but in the end, only one sight registers: two dark eyes.

"Look at me." He must come closer, because the shadows recede, allowing me to make his face out clearly.

Just like that, I stop inhaling what little air my lungs managed to suck in.

It will never cease to amaze me how this man can turn something like confusion into the most devastatingly violent thing to witness. His jaw is a chiseled line, his mouth stretched tautly. Sweat glues his shirt to his body, his muscles rippling as his hands wrestle his cock beneath the zipper.

I know, even before he says the words, that this isn't over.

"Tell me to release you."

Shivers run down my spine at the strained tone. I'm still on the hook: still naked, my arms stretched above my head. I can feel his seed drying on my inner thigh and our sweat slicking my skin.

Without the high from the sex, the position is agony. Unbearable. Dried, my lips spring apart. "P-please."

Satisfied, he muscles in, cupping one massive hand against my ass. "Hold on to me."

A whine rips from my throat as the tension in my body suddenly snaps. He's already there to catch me when I fall, holding me close. I do my best to dig my nails into the fabric of his shirt, but even that seems damn near impossible. My muscles are jelly. Breathing is a struggle.

I should be terrified, I think. It can't be good to be this disjointed. So dizzy. So tired. So fucking *real*.

For the first time in my life, there is no fog threatening to descend. Just cold, harsh reality.

And he gave it to me—this man who lifts me like I weigh nothing, cradling my body in his arms.

Seconds later, he lays me onto something soft. Through heavy-lidded eyes, I recognize his second room.

"Are you in pain?"

The knowing tone in his voice quickens my already racing heartbeat.

"Yes," I admit into the silken sheets.

His next words come thickly. "Tell me where."

I flinch at the question, unsure of how to respond. Would *my fucking self-worth* be an adequate answer? I doubt it. So I improvise and blurt out an area on my actual body.

"My back…"

I hear him grunt in acknowledgment. Footsteps follow, but I'm too damn exhausted to turn my head and see their destination. I just have to wait and listen. Something that sounds like a drawer opens and closes. More footsteps.

When he's close again, my nostrils flare, catching the familiar aroma of his musk mingled with something sharper. Spice. It's like my body knows when he's near before I even do. It tenses up, every nerve on high alert, before the mattress dips beneath his weight, and his breath fans the back of my neck.

"Spread out your arms," he tells me.

When I obey, a warm substance falls onto the middle of my back and I have to smother the urge to shudder. Whatever it is feels like liquid. Hot. Oil? Something heavier descends before I can be sure, rubbing the substance into my skin. His hand? His *palm*, each finger fanning out along my spine, nudging tense muscle underneath.

I suck in a breath as he presses hard, setting off a chain reaction of sore muscles and aching nerves. He performs the same manipulative stroke three more times before I actually realize what he's doing. Massaging. Tugging. Pulling. I'm at his mercy, and my brain anxiously tracks each touch, anticipating the moment a fingernail might stab through my skin. Would that ruin this? Make it better?

"You will have some muscle tenderness for the next few days," he warns me without an ounce of guilt lurking in his voice. "Next time, I will better prepare you before using the hook."

I stop breathing, hung up on so many implications of that statement.

"I *will* do this to you again," he promises, reading my mind. There's a slight tremor in his voice: impatience. Like he can't wait to string me up a second time.

Tonight? I press my cheek against the sheet beneath it and tell myself that I wouldn't want him to. *Because...*

"Do you know why you came back to me?" he asks, interrupting my quest for an answer. His free hand sinks into my hair, wrenching my head back so that I can face him directly. "Do you? You said it once. Say it again."

I swallow hard and resist the urge to shake my head. Lying —that's Melanie's trick. The one thing I've always been able to fall back on. You lie to the patsy you're planning to screw over. You lie to yourself. To do otherwise is fucking suicide.

It should be easy to lie now, but looking at him…I just nod once.

"Say it," he prompts, tugging on my scalp when I don't comply quickly enough.

Freedom should be a good thing, but my body doesn't think so. Both lungs seize. "Because…"

I trail off.

He waits.

In the end, I guess there's only one real answer. "Because you make me feel wanted."

A low sound rumbles from his chest. It's only when he throws his head back that I can put a name to what it was: a laugh, unlike any I've ever heard. Beautiful, fucked-up noise.

Rather than say anything else, he releases his grip on my hair and continues his massage, moving along my lower back before digging into my arms.

I can't escape the mental comparison to how he handles his tools: wiping them down after a brutal sculpting session, rubbing oil into each scratch and imperfection.

"Wanted," he finally echoes after one last manipulation of my wrist. His tone is less gruff. I guess he's agreeing with me. "That is one way to put it."

The mattress shifts as he stands and circles the bed toward the direction I'm facing. Step, by step, by step…

"But I will tell you the real reason why." He stops just beyond my line of sight. While I stiffen in anticipation, his shadow falls over me, painting the edges of my vision black. "The real world doesn't keep you here. Not always. It can be too…harsh. Too cold." He's speaking from experience, his words losing their polish again for a brief second. "You go numb."

My hands twitch weakly at my sides, desperate to clamp over my ears. He shouldn't be making sense. Not now, when I'm too tired to counter him. Those weeks alone flicker across the inside of my skull like a slideshow of emotion. How it felt—or more like how cutting myself *didn't* make me feel.

"Look at me."

I must have closed my eyes, because they flutter open as something brushes my chin. His finger. With surprising gentleness, he uses it to steer my face up in his direction. Darkness has swallowed his pupils again, but this time, he doesn't seem inhuman. Just fucking insane.

"I can make it better…can't I?" His voice is rough, like he's unsure of the words even as they leave his mouth. Like…he wants them to be true. "In a way that even you cannot."

He nods toward my wrist and I instinctively draw the hand closer to my side, bunching my fingers up to hide the cuts slashed across my palm. I can't disguise the other marks though. Ironically, they look even worse than the mess he's made of my skin. His marks are precise blows from a chisel. Mine are just sloppy. Not artful.

And that's just it: He turns agony into *art*.

"Coming back to me... You know what this means, don't you, *kotyonok*?" His head is cocked to the side, those eyes unreadable for once.

I have to take a risk and guess what emotion might be filling them now. I know anger on him. Confusion. Hate.

Maybe this is something different: pity.

"No," I croak, the truth.

Rather than punish me, he strokes his hand along my cheek. "I will release you, and you will stay because you want to."

My eyes start to burn. Blinking just makes it worse and hot liquid spills onto my cheeks. *Damn it.*

Slowly, I nod. Swallow. "Y-yes..."

Watching him this way, I finally see a shadow of the creature he must have been on stage. Tall. Imposing. Blond hair wild, eyes blazing, body radiating tension.

No wonder that little redhead looked so eager to be near him, even if it only meant being flogged. No wonder the entire fucking room of people stopped to watch him at work. If I wanted to take pity on myself in this moment, I'd go a step further: *No wonder you've gone fucking insane.*

It's impossible to judge your own mental psyche when looking at him. He's fucking psychotic, but he doesn't even begin to hide it.

He paints the world with it, not giving a damn for the lives he might stain with his twisted brand of madness.

"Sleep," he tells me once he finally reaches the door, feeling along the wall to shut the light off. He doesn't have to say the rest.

You'll need it.

CHAPTER TWENTY-TWO

He doesn't take me back to the suite.

I'm eerily familiar with our destination anyway: a desolate, dank parking garage. Dread congeals in my throat, making it harder to breathe as he exits the car. The door slams after him—and it all clicks.

He made up his mind, all right: If he can't fight for me, he'll destroy me.

"No." The refusal slips out of me unbidden, impossible to bite back. My fingers grip the handle tight while I try to find the lock. "N-No—"

"Come." His voice reaches me through metal and glass, faint but still laced with authority. There is nothing in his tone to give me a hint of what he's feeling or why he's brought me here.

But it's obvious: to kill me for good this time.

"Just let me go," I croak. "Please let me go—"

"*Kotyonok...*" He advances toward the door and wrenches it open from the outside as I cling to the handle. "Come with me."

He pries my hand loose, yanking me to my feet, and my brain goes blank.

"No!" I lash out, nails drawn, desperate for any part of him I can reach. Skin. Cotton. Anything. I kick and I hit with everything I fucking have.

But he's stone, impossible to outmaneuver.

"Enough!" He grabs my wrists, pinning them both to the hood of the car. The harder I try to escape, the tighter his grip becomes. "You have nothing to fear." He frowns, as if the thought only just occurred to him.

I can barely contain my scoff even as he releases me and holds his hand out for me to take.

"Do I really need to say it after everything else that's happened tonight?" Irritation makes his tone even harsher than anger—but his expression softens in the same instant. "Fine. I will not hurt you here. I need you to trust me."

Panting, I eye his fingers and consider running. Trust? Why, when all he's done is prove why I shouldn't? My blood pistons through me, making my entire body jolt with each frantic beat of my heart. If I listen hard enough, the thrum sounds like a warning. *Run. Run. Run.*

"Can you give me that?" he wonders, consuming my focus. I look up, unnerved by the uncertainty I see in his gaze. As if, for the first time, he can't predict what I'll do. He's just as unsure of me as I am of him.

"Come," he prompts, flexing his fingers. "I'm asking for your trust."

This time, I reach out and let him grasp my hand. He tugs, guiding me step by step down that dank, dark hallway. My nostrils flare. It still smells like rust, but now an even worse stench lurks underneath. Something rotten? Decaying.

The closer we come to the back room the more sweat slicks my fingers and it's easier than ever to slip from his grip if I have to.

Even his reassurance can push me only so far.

I stop dead in my tracks just beyond the doorway as my eyes warily trace the interior. The tarp is gone, at least. But in the center of the space lies a reddish stain someone tried very, very hard to get up with bleach, if the acrid stench left behind is any indicator.

They failed.

"Come here." From the doorway, Maxim watches me, his face partially hidden by shadow. "I will not hurt you here," he stresses. "So trust me. Come."

His eyes track my approach. When I'm close enough, he captures my entire hand in one of his own, his eyes honing in on my heaving chest.

Only now do I realize we're not alone.

A man lies in a far corner of the room, beyond the view from the doorway. Someone stripped him naked, and my stomach threatens to crawl up my throat as a sliver of light gives his flesh definition. A rainbow of violent, grim color. Purplish bruises and red, gaping wounds form a collage that covers him from head to toe. Some of the cuts bleed and ooze, still fresh.

The stench assaulting my nostrils warns that whoever he is, he's been here for days. Beaten for days…

My gaze fixates on a particularly nasty row of scratches along his shoulder and both eyes widen. It looks as if someone dug their nails in with all their might without giving a fuck as to the damage they'd cause.

"Back so soon…Maxi?" A hoarse, ragged sound fills the room. A laugh. *His.* He's alive. *Sevastyn?*

I flinch back, wrenching out of Maxim's reach. "What did you—"

"Look at me," Maxim commands. His hand latches onto my chin, giving me no choice but to obey. "You wanted to know why I left…" He waits until I nod.

"I went to Russia and met with some of my uncle's old acquaintances. Some of them were hostile to me. But others had axes to grind." His eyes flash, displaying every ounce of ruthlessness I know he possesses. "In the end, most gave me their loyalty. So if Anatoli wants retribution…he can have his war."

My head spins. "But—"

"As for *you*." He returns his attention to Sevastyn. "I thought even a dog like you should be shown mercy before you die. I'll let you plead for your life, even." He cuts his gaze back to me. "So beg her for it."

I sway. Maxim's lips continue to move but all I can hear is the whoosh of air leaving my chest and the thrum of my pulse hammering through my eardrums. I try to speak. Refuse. Scream—anything.

The moment my lips part, more maniacal laughter drowns out whatever I intend to say.

"Mercy?" Sevastyn wonders, his voice wracked with pain. "For me, Maxim? Or her?" His eyes seek mine out, red and swollen but gleaming. Burning. "You think I'm the monster? He'll destroy you worse than I ever could. You never could protect your toys, could you, Maxi?" He spits out each word, spraying blood. "You are pathetic. Still just a soft, pansy little fa—"

"Enough!" Maxim lunges, a blur of shadow, and something silver arches through the air. Sevastyn grunts and I turn away—but not fast enough to avoid seeing the blood splattering the gray floor.

And then silence descends like a noose.

I can't move. My eyes sear with the horror of what I've witnessed, but in a sick way I can still pretend that it was just a trick of the light. Or a nightmare.

That this isn't real.

But the man crouched before me *is*, and for some twisted reason my brain doesn't shy from his violence. Not the blood streaking his pale hands, or the harshness in the grunt he releases, throaty and raw as the metal object in his grip falls to the floor.

"He's wrong," he murmurs, rising to his feet. "Protect you? I'll do so much fucking more than that." The air hitches in my throat as he faces me, sweeping his gaze along my body. "I've thought of so many ways. So many ways to mark you. I've considered them all. Branding," he says musingly as he wipes his scarlet fingers onto the front of his expensive slacks, "with ink or with fire. A collar. A leash. Something so that the world knows you are *mine*."

That dark gleam in his eye greedily strips me down to the bone. Like he could devour me, body and soul.

"But none of those methods were enough," he continues while advancing on me another step.

I stagger in the opposite direction out of pure instinct, but my back strikes the wall and there is no escape.

"It isn't enough that the world knows you are mine, if you still have doubts."

Shaking his head, he approaches a table overrun with stone dust and worn tools in the corner and lifts something from the piled-up chaos.

"Here." He extends his hand. Warily, I wrestle my limbs into submission and cross over to him.

My fingers shake, grasping at the air as he drops a single object onto my palm. It's small, whatever it is. And yet oddly heavy. I almost can't bear to unfurl my fingers. So I don't. I tremble, observed by the man before me, and for some reason he allows me just a few moments of disobedience.

"Look at it, *kotyonok*," he commands finally.

The tone of his voice snaps me into action and I crane my neck down while peeling my fingers apart.

A small circlet of black marble rests on my palm. Streaks of silver embedded into the stone catch the light like stars in the night sky. It's beautiful. I can admit that—despite the way my stomach sinks to my toes as a gasp escapes my lips.

There in the center of it, etched in gold, is a single name, shining with ownership. MAXIM.

"You wear it when you are ready," he tells me. "When you can give me your trust... Can you give me that? Can you prove him wrong?"

"H-How?" I rasp.

"It is simple." He almost seems to shrug despite the tension radiating off him conveying anything but nonchalance. "Francesca Marconi must die—"

"What?" I rock back on my heels but he grabs my arm before I can attempt to run.

"You give me everything," he says, tightening his grip as he braces against me from behind. "Your body. Your life. Your name..." His fingers grasp mine, curling them around the ring I'm still holding.

"And you take mine." He breathes heavily against my throat, painting me with fire in every exhale. "As a Koslov, I can protect you. Forever."

And *now* I know exactly why he's brought me here. In shock, I eye our entwined fingers, his rough and tanned, mine trembling and pale.

Ink.

Blood.

Marble.

They are all just symbols—but a man like Maxim doesn't mark his ownership with something so simple. A man like him won't just claim any soul he craves. It must be offered.

With complete surrender.

~ Continues in Book 3 Surrender ~
Now Available!

A WORD FROM THE AUTHOR

Hey there!

Thank you so much for reading! If you enjoyed the story, please leave a review and recommend the book to any friend you think would love this twisted world. You'd have my eternal gratitude. Even a short sentence goes a long way!

Then, come join the rest of us dark romance lovers in my Facebook Group where you can get snippets, sneak peeks of upcoming books and even help vote on aspects of future novels.

Come to the dark side:
https://www.facebook.com/groups/lanasbeautifulmonsters/

WANT MORE STUFF TO READ?
Join my newsletter and get a **free book**! Plus, you get to stay updated with any new releases, random giveaways and exclusive sneak peeks!
https://www.lanaskybooks.com/newsletter

Other Novels: https://lanaskybooks.com/

ABOUT THE AUTHOR

Lana Sky is a reclusive writer in the United States who spends most of her time daydreaming about complex male characters and parenting her Cockapoo Joey. She writes dark, twisted romance across several genres. Her titles include everything from mafia romance to vampires.

facebook.com/AuthorLanaSky

twitter.com/lanasky101

amazon.com/author/lanasky

pinterest.com/lanasky101

goodreads.com/lanasky

instagram.com/lanasky101

bookbub.com/authors/lana-sky